I'm a

So a
Spider
What?

13

OKINA BABA

Illustration by
TSUKASA KIRYU

YEN
ON

New York

So I'm a Spider, So What?, Vol. 13

Okina Baba

Translation by Jenny McKeon
Cover art by Tsukasa Kiryu

KUMO DESUGA, NANIKA? Vol. 13
©Okina Baba, Tsukasa Kiryu 2020
First published in Japan in 2020 by KADOKAWA CORPORATION, Tokyo.
English translation rights arranged with KADOKAWA CORPORATION, Tokyo, through TUTTLE-MORI AGENCY, INC., Tokyo.

English translation © 2022 by Yen Press, LLC

Yen On
150 West 30th Street, 19th Floor
New York, NY 10001

Visit us at yenpress.com
facebook.com/yenpress
twitter.com/yenpress
yenpress.tumblr.com
instagram.com/yenpress

First Yen On Edition: January 2022

Yen On is an imprint of Yen Press, LLC.
The Yen On name and logo are trademarks of Yen Press, LLC.

Library of Congress Cataloging-in-Publication Data
Names: Baba, Okina, author. | Kiryu, Tsukasa, illustrator. | McKeon, Jenny, translator.
Title: So I'm a spider, so what? / Okina Baba ; illustration by Tsukasa Kiryu ; translation by Jenny McKeon.
Other titles: Kumo desuga nanika. English | So I am a spider, so what?
Description: First Yen On edition. | New York, NY : Yen On, 2017–
Identifiers: LCCN 2017034911 | ISBN 9780316412896 (v. 1 : pbk.) | ISBN 9780316442886 (v. 2 : pbk.) | ISBN 9780316442909 (v. 3 : pbk.) | ISBN 9780316442916 (v. 4 : pbk.) | ISBN 9781975301941 (v. 5 : pbk.) | ISBN 9781975301965 (v. 6 : pbk.) | ISBN 9781975301989 (v. 7 : pbk.) | ISBN 9781975398996 (v. 8 : pbk.) | ISBN 9781975310349 (v. 9 : pbk.) | ISBN 9781975310363 (v. 10 : pbk.) | ISBN 9781975310387 (v. 11 : pbk.) | ISBN 9781975321826 (v. 12 : pbk.) | ISBN 9781975339852 (v. 13 ; pbk.)
Subjects: CYAC: Magic—Fiction. | Spiders—Fiction. | Monsters—Fiction. | Prisons—Fiction. | Escapes—Fiction. | Fantasy.
Classification: LCC PZ7.1.O44 So 2017 | DDC [Fic]—dc23
LC record available at https://lccn.loc.gov/2017034911

ISBNs: 978-1-9753-3985-2 (paperback)
       978-1-9753-3986-9 (ebook)

10 9 8 7 6 5 4 3 2 1

LSC-C

Printed in the United States of America

contents

Exterminating Monsters for a Living

"RUOOOOOOHHHR!!"

An otherworldly roar echoes all around me.

If I had to say, I guess the silhouette producing it looks sort of like a whale?

But that's just a wild guess based on the general shape. From what I've seen, its actual appearance is a far cry from any whale.

To be honest, all they really have in common is a short but wide body.

We're on land right now anyway, so a sea creature like a whale wouldn't be here in the first place.

In fact, do this world's oceans even have whales?

While I'm distracted with these stupid thoughts, the whale monster gets engulfed in explosions.

"RUOOOHH! RUOOOOHRRR!!"

The great big thing thrashes around angrily.

That alone is enough to crack open the earth around it and send shock waves in every direction.

Its body is huge, which is the other reason I compared it to a whale.

Seriously, it's freaking huge. Makes me want to say, *We're gonna need a bigger boat.*

When something's got that much mass, it's automatically a major threat.

So if I were to try again to explain this whale monster's appearance, well… it's still really hard to put into words.

The resemblance to a whale is all I can think of.

It's hard to tell where the head ends and its body begins.

Really, the face is basically just a mouth—no eyes or nose that I can see.

And the mouth in question really just looks like a big hole.

Maybe it'd be more accurate to call it a giant worm monster or something?

Yeah, it's got one of those huge yawning maws.

But this thing's not a worm monster, and it's got the limbs to prove it.

Its front limbs are like giant fins, and the ones it has in the back are like fish tails, attached to the end opposite the giant mouth.

So I guess...yeah. Overall, it still looks like a whale.

But I think it'd be a serious stretch to call this thing a whale!

"RUOOOOHHHH!"

Another roar bounces out of the whale monster's cavernous mouth.

"Oh, be quiet!"

Vampy slashes at the creature to interrupt its roaring.

Her broadsword makes contact with its flabby gray skin but fails to cut through.

"Tch!"

As Vampy scowls, the whale monster lashes out with its fins.

Her body goes flying almost comically.

The monster leans forward in preparation to jump after Vampy.

But that slight movement is all it takes.

It's thread.

Too thin for such a giant creature to notice without careful inspection, and now it's wrapped around the whale monster's entire body.

The net is being pulled tight by the puppet spiders, who have fanned out in all directions.

Together, the four of them have completely trapped the beast.

"RUOOOH!"

The whale monster emits a short roar.

A burst of chill air shoots out from the monster, freezing the thread and shattering it.

But then a single sword suddenly appears, slicing through the air.

It explodes. Flames shoot everywhere.

For an instant, the heat of the explosion crashes against the whale monster's cold blast, but the latter wins out.

This thing's stupid strong...

I guess that's why it's a legendary-class monster.

Yes, that's right: This thing's danger level is apparently legendary, meaning humans consider it unbeatable.

A single legendary-class monster is supposed to be strong enough to destroy an entire nation.

This whale monster is one of those.

It's a living legend that's survived in the northern reaches of the demon realm for ages, hidden in a wasteland where no one dares tread.

What is its name again...?

I feel like it was super long and hard to pronounce...

Hypo-something-or-other?

...Yep, let's just stick with whale monster!

While I'm racking my brains trying to remember the stupid thing's name, the battle rages on.

The lineup this time consists of Vampy, Mr. Oni, the puppet spiders, and Mera.

They're all crazy fighters, and way stronger than the average human.

Together, they can even take on a legendary monster.

Although in terms of stats alone, the puppet spiders count as legendary-class, too.

But of course, *legendary-class* covers a pretty wide range.

For instance, even though they're all legendary-class, there's a world of difference between the puppet spiders and, say, Mother.

By the same token, the whale monster is far stronger than the puppet spiders.

I can't use Appraisal anymore, so I don't know the exact details, but I'd estimate that its stats probably average around 15,000. If the puppet spiders' average is a little over 10,000, I guess that makes the difference a multiplier of 1.5 or so.

The puppet spiders alone wouldn't be able to beat this thing one-on-one.

Of course, that's why we decided to attack with a bigger group.

But in this world, you can't predict the outcome of a battle based solely on stats and numbers.

There are other important factors, like skill quality and type matchup.

On that front, the whale monster is a fairly formidable opponent.

All spider monsters, including the puppet spiders, are weak against ice.

It's not as bad as fire, but it's still not something you wanna see if you walk on eight legs.

Plus, Vampy specializes in Ice Magic.

Using ice against ice isn't gonna do very much.

In fact, I'd be willing to bet that the whale monster has a nullification skill for ice by now, meaning it wouldn't do squat.

And judging by the way Vampy's sword bounced right off earlier, it must be pretty resistant to cutting attacks, too.

In other words, this is a bad adversary for both the puppet spiders and Vampy.

Which would theoretically mean it's Mera and Mr. Oni's time to shine, but...

They're both clearly not strong enough.

Mera's always been the runt of the litter and all...

I mean, he works hard, y'know?

Considering he used to be a plain old human, I'd say it's amazing that he can even hold his own in this earth-shaking battle.

He's been working really, really hard.

The sad news is that alone isn't enough to win in a situation like this.

He doesn't have any way of doing real damage to the whale monster.

Mera seems to be aware of that, too. He's just focusing on Healing Magic and giving support however he can.

As for Mr. Oni, well, at least he has attacks that work.

Like those exploding swords and stuff.

But even then, the pure insanity of the whale monster's stats means he's not really getting anywhere.

That cold-air blast did totally cancel out the explosion after all...

So basically, all seven of them are just barely enough to be an even match.

Damn, whale monster, you scary.

I guess it was bound to be super strong, though.

This monster is so ancient, we don't even know how long it's been here.

According to demon legends, it's been holed up in the north since before people started counting time.

Even the Demon Lord says she doesn't know how long it's been around, so it's gotta be pretty damn old.

And time equals strength in this world.

Just look at the Demon Lord if you need proof.

Live long enough and you'll build up lots of experience points.

And naturally, your skill levels will go up a whole bunch, too.

Not to mention, this northern part of the demon realm is incredibly cold, although it's still not as bad as the Mystic Mountains.

It's a tough place for anything to call home.

So any creature that's survived here for ages and ages definitely isn't gonna be a pushover.

I've heard demons actually have a saying that goes something like, "Don't wander up north, or Hypo-whatever is gonna getcha!"

All that means this thing's strong and ancient enough to be a bona fide legend.

Oh? Vampy is attacking with her acid now.

The bloodred spray flies toward the monster, melting through the tough hide that no one has managed to even scratch yet.

"RUOOOOOOOOOOOOOOOOHH!"

The whale gives its longest roar yet.

I guess that must've worked.

Of course, our leviathan foe isn't just gonna take it lying down, and it lunges at Vampy mouth-first.

Vampy dodges it easily, and the whale monster ends up kissing the ground instead.

But it doesn't just crash stupidly; it cuts through the ground as easily as butter, the earth disappearing into its mouth.

Then the whale monster rears back its head, and the dirt rockets back out of its mouth in a muddy stream.

Actually, is it a stream or a breath attack?

Whatever it is, it's heading straight for Vampy.

"Wha—?!"

"Young Miss?!"

Vampy gets swallowed up by the sand.

Eh, she's not gonna die that easily.

Plus, Mera's already heading over to help her.

More importantly, I know I said that thing isn't a worm before, but maybe it is kinda related to a worm after all?

What kind of evolutionary line would produce a freaky creature like this, exactly?

It's a puzzle all right, but there's no point thinking too hard about the mysteries of life.

The main problem at hand is whether we can beat the thing or not.

If you're wondering why we're fighting this whale monster in the first place, it's so we can collect its energy.

See, there are other legendary-class monsters lurking in various uninhabited areas.

They're all creatures just like the whale monster that've lived for so long, they've become too powerful for humans to take on.

The monsters in this world are programmed to aggressively attack humans.

That's so they can either get defeated by humans or defeat the humans, growing stronger and perpetuating a cycle of dying and killing, killing and dying—all to provide the system with a steady stream of energy.

But once in a blue moon, there are monsters like this whale thing that keep surviving until humans can't kill them anymore.

If these walking natural disasters aggressively attacked humans all the time, humanity would be done for in no time.

That's why once a monster surpasses a certain level of strength, it's programmed to aggressively avoid humans instead.

And that's basically how legendary-class monsters work.

Although of course, it's really just a strong mental suggestion to do that, so there are some exceptions that attack humans anyway.

Historically, monsters that act out usually get defeated by heroes, demon lords, or other legendary figures after a life-and-death battle.

If they were left alone, they would be a real threat to mankind's continued existence after all. Of course people are gonna put their lives on the line to get rid of them.

Of course, the scariest monsters might get dealt with by Güli-güli (aka Black) or the current Demon Lord without anyone else knowing.

Anyway, since these legendary-class monsters have accumulated so many experience points, they create a huge amount of energy when you kill them.

So before we ultimately destroy the system once and for all, we're trying to add on as much energy as possible by hunting down legendary-class monsters.

Plus, it helps level up Vampy and the others.

There'd be less energy loss if I just mopped the floor with these guys myself, though…since some of the energy becomes experience for our crew to level up.

But really, that's well within our margin of error.

We decided it would be best right now to prepare for the final battle by improving our allies' strength, which is why this group is taking care of the legendary monster hunting.

But if things start to get dicey, I'll step in and crush 'em, of course.

Yep. Legendary-class or not, I can win without a problem the way I am now.

And since I'm watching over them, this is actually a pretty safe method of level-grinding.

Luckily, there hasn't been any need for me to step in yet.

They've already defeated several legendary-class monsters as strong as this whale monster—and some were stronger.

A lot of monsters that were on their way to becoming legendary-class, too.

Of course, since we have four genuine legendary-class monsters on our side in the form of the puppet spiders, these would-be legendaries are no challenge at all.

In terms of strength, Vampy and Mr. Oni qualify as legendary-class, too.

And Mera… Well, he's doing his best as a supporter! Yeah!

Listen, you've got it all wrong! Mera isn't weak at all! These opponents are just too strong!

I mean, his stats average around 5,000 now.

That's higher than Araba, you know? And if he's stronger than Araba, he's definitely not weak!

It's just that the opponents we're fighting are even stronger than that…

As their title implies, legendary-class monsters are the stuff of myths and…well…legends.

They're not kidding when they say it's impossible for humans to beat them.

Mera himself is insanely strong from the perspective of any human.

But even if he's way out of their league, it's not impossible for them to deal with him...

'Cause in the big battle with the humans a while back, Mera was forced to retreat.

Honestly, someone as strong as Mera getting driven away was a biiig surprise.

Even with an overwhelming difference in stats, it's possible to make up for the gap with numbers and sheer determination.

Just like how we're taking on this big guy right now.

As Vampy's acid melts through the whale monster's hide, the puppet spiders mercilessly rain poison on the newly exposed flesh, and once that slows it down, Mr. Oni comes in with his exploding swords.

Are you guys demons or what?!

...Yeah, I guess that's exactly what the three of them are, more or less.

And the other four are spiders, sooo yeah.

Yep, they're still spiders all right... It's easy to forget since they look just like humans at this point, but the puppet spiders really are spiders.

Which means of course they're gonna have poison.

They haven't had much of a chance to show off the full range of their abilities, since their opponents just haven't been strong enough to merit it. But the truth is, in terms of the sheer number of different cards they can play, the puppet spiders are pretty damn dangerous even by legendary-class standards.

They've got threads and poison to boot, plus their humanoid puppet bodies can use weapons and martial arts.

Their stats might be on the lower side for legendary-class, but their combat strategies are varied enough to more than make up for it.

Although the fact that they're on the "lower side" really is terrifying in itself.

But even these terrifying legendary-class monsters are now nothing more than hunting fodder for us.

The whale monster's giant body slowly tips to the side.

Before long, it slams into the ground with a mighty *crash*, sending tremors through the earth.

"Ugggh...I need a bath..."

"Excellent work, Young Miss."

"Good job."

Now thoroughly covered in dirt, Vampy seems more exhausted than satisfied.

Mera comforts her by praising her efforts, while Mr. Oni quietly nods at both of them.

The puppet spider sisters all high-five one another.

That whale monster had fairly high stats and resistances, but once you deal with those, I guess it wasn't that big of a deal.

Its main attack methods consisted of sucking things into its mouth and spitting them out at high speeds, like a certain pink puffball creature.

Other than that, its only moves were producing freezing air and using its huge body to thrash around.

Since its attacks were nothing special compared to its defense, we didn't have too much trouble.

That's just compared to other legendary-class monsters, though. Normally, one of these guys could easily take out an entire army, I'm sure.

Still lost in thought over all this, I walk over to the fallen whale monster.

I was watching from a slight distance, so I'm a little far away. Sure, I could teleport there in an instant, but it's good for my health to walk once in a while!

"Ah."

Vampy notices me approaching.

Then she looks back and forth between me and the whale monster, then at her own giant sword.

Oh, I don't like where this is going.

"Say, I don't suppose…"

"No."

I shut Vampy down before she can finish her wheedling request.

"Come on, please? For me?"

She tilts her head and bats her eyes at me coquettishly.

Ugh. Ever since she learned how to make boys wait on her hand and foot at the demon academy, she's picked up weird habits like this.

You really think that cutesy crap is going to work on me?!

"I told you, no."

"Boooo."

That adorable little pout isn't getting you anywhere, missy!

Besides, I really can't do it anyway.

In case you're wondering, Vampy is asking for permission to harvest materials from this whale monster to make her weapon stronger.

Vampy's broadsword was made from the claw of a legendary-class monster called Fenrir and enhanced with the scale of another legendary monster, the ice dragon Nia.

Thanks to all that, it's basically a super-weapon, with incredible sharpness, high durability, and even imbued with the Ice element.

The whale monster is Ice aligned, too, meaning it'd probably be pretty compatible with the broadsword.

But I don't even have! The ability! To process stuff like that!

In the first place, it was Black who modified the sword the first time, not me.

Just because I'm a god, too, doesn't mean I can do everything he can do.

"Sophia, you sure you want to mix that thing with your sword?"

Noticing Sophia's sulking, Mr. Oni throws me a lifeline.

He points at the whale monster; it was already hard enough to describe, but now its blubbery hide has been melted by acid, making it even look even more alien.

Honestly, it's super gross.

"……"

Vampy looks at it and falls silent.

Then she slides away from me, giving up.

I guess she doesn't want to mix something that gross with her beloved broadsword after all.

The fact that she didn't think of this in the first place is so typical. Vampy never thinks before she acts, which is also how she ended up causing so many problems at school.

Well, I guess that doesn't matter right now.

I go back to my business, which is teleporting the whale monster's body to a separate dimension.

When you're dealing with a legendary monster's corpse, it still has a fair amount of energy even after its soul has vacated.

The soul gets collected by the system, but the body just stays there. And it'd be silly to just let that energy go to waste, so we put it to good use.

When I send the corpse into my storage dimension, it gets eaten by my little clones, and they absorb its energy.

Of course, we could send that energy into the system, too, in theory...

But I do want to use some of it to bolster our forces.

Now that's how you make effective use of resources!

Even if it looks nasty, it's still a nutrient-rich food source that provides lots of energy!

So quit looking at me like that, Vampy!

Once I teleported Vampy and the others back to the Demon Lord's castle, I headed over to a human fortress.

Or I guess I should say a *former* human fortress.

Fort Okun originally belonged to the humans, but the Second Army conquered it in that big battle a little while ago.

Hrm. Then again, it might be more accurate to say the monkeys sent in by the Second Army conquered it, not the Second Army themselves.

Remember those monkeys that gave me so much trouble in the Great Elroe Labyrinth?

Well, they also live in the Mystic Mountains, so Commander Boobs of the Second Army lured them in and sicced 'em on Fort Okun.

The annoying thing about those monkeys is that if you kill even one, the rest of them will keep coming after you in waves...

Turns out it just happened to be the tail end of their breeding season, too, so there were tons of monkeys around, and they totally trashed the fortress.

That's how the Second Army won without a single casualty.

There's just one problem, though.

Namely, the monkeys. They decided to keep Fort Okun as their base...

Chasing them out should really be the Second Army's job, but slippery ol' Boobs managed to sidestep that responsibility.

Makes sense, I guess. She wouldn't want to bring down a fortress unscathed only to lose a bunch of people fighting those monkeys. That might even produce more casualties than fighting the humans would've.

I mean, these monkeys are the ones who beat the humans.

Luckily, they're just sitting around in the fortress and not trying to attack the demons. The Second Army has just been camping out nearby, ostensibly to keep an eye on them.

Although it's pretty damn obvious that Boobs just wants to stay out of the Demon Lord's sight, y'know?

I mean, she's terrified of the big boss.

She's probably hoping she can just hide out here on monkey watch indefinitely, I bet.

Not on my watch!

"I have written orders from the Demon Lord."

Phelmina calmly hands Boobs the letter, then explains its contents shortly.

"It says to return home right away."

Boobs accepts the letter silently, her brow creasing as she opens it.

Aside from a few formalities, it says just about exactly what Phelmina described—"Come back now"—and that's about it.

There aren't many extra embellishments, either, so it only takes a moment to read.

"But we have to monitor that fortress…"

"We in the Tenth Army will be taking over that role."

Boobs tries to give an excuse, but Phelmina shuts her down. Boobs glowers at her.

"We'll need some time to prepare…"

"Lady Sanatoria." Phelmina coolly interrupts with her name as Boobs keeps trying to give excuses. "The Demon Lord has ordered you to return at once. If you disobey her…I'm sure you realize what will happen, yes?"

Boobs turns pale.

Not long after, she starts moving real quickly.

Her army gets it together in no time flat, and they're on their way home before the day is out.

Talk about lightning speed!

She's actually a fairly gifted leader when it comes down to it.

She's good at giving orders, and she did take down a fortress without any casualties, even if it was by way of a crafty plan.

But the thing is, she's just kind of a wimp.

I mean, she's only moving this incredibly fast because she's terrified of the Demon Lord.

Except the Demon Lord is gonna be waiting for her when she gets back anyway.

You gotta love the way she sets herself up for a fall by being too crafty for her own good.

But whatever does or doesn't happen to Boobs isn't my problem.

Once the Second Army gets out of here and there's no one around to watch, that's where my job begins.

"Well then, Tenth Army. We will now commence the operation to conquer Fort Okun."

Phelmina leads the Tenth Army toward the fortress.

She made it sound like we were going to take over monitoring the fortress, but we're not the kind of boys and girls to just sit around watching.

No, our goal is to wipe out these monkeys.

Following Phelmina's orders, the white-robed soldiers march closer to the fortress.

The monkeys notice this and start throwing rocks, but my unit dodges them all easily.

Not that they'd take any damage even if they did get hit.

After all, those white clothes were specially made by yours truly, out of my own thread!

Their high defense is guaranteed.

I *am* technically the commander, after all.

I figured if I'm gonna be in charge of a unit, I better give them the best armor I can muster, so I made some top-notch stuff!

And yes, of course they're decked out with the finest equipment, too.

Sure enough, once they reach the fortress, they start climbing the steep walls in no time flat.

Ignoring the rocks being thrown at them, they quickly make their way inside and begin the assault.

Although it's so one-sided, I'd really call it more of a slaughter.

Those monkeys are definitely a pain, but that's only because of their overwhelming strength in numbers. The biggest challenge in fighting them is that they just keep swarming, no matter how many of them you take down.

But no matter how big their numbers, there's still gotta be a limit.

You just have to kill 'em until they run out, like I once did in the Great Elroe Labyrinth.

The monkeys in this fortress have already lost a bunch of their numbers in the fight against the humans.

And each individual monkey isn't that strong on its own.

With all these factors in play, the group I trained can definitely come out on top.

The Tenth Army is a part of the demon army that falls under my command.

It's a job the Demon Lord dropped in my lap a few years ago while preparing for the big war against the humans. Yeah, she kinda forced me to do it.

But really, it's because I didn't have a proper position in the demon army, and the Tenth Army didn't actually exist as anything more than a name on paper at the time. She figured it was a perfect fit and appointed me commander.

The demon army has always had seven armies, but the Eighth, Ninth, and Tenth Armies weren't actually functional groups at all. There just weren't enough demons to fill the ranks, what with the population shortage.

But between the Demon Lord's expansion policies, purging the rebels, structural reform, and all that jazz, she decided to form ten proper armies.

So she appointed Mr. Oni as the commander of the Eighth Army and filled the ranks with the personal armies of some lords who'd committed fraud and stuff like that.

Basically, it's a bunch of soldiers who've been reduced to slaves only fit for suicide missions.

Since these guys are essentially disposable, Mr. Oni wound up using his exploding swords to blow up tons of people in the big battle, including his own troops.

The Ninth Army is a totally different situation; the soldiers are definitely…outsiders, to say the least.

After all, the Ninth Commander is Black, aka Güli-güli.

In order to keep an eye on me and the Demon Lord while aiding our efforts, he became the official Ninth Army Commander so he could hang out in the demon realm.

As for his army, it's made up of his underlings—dragons and wyrms pretending to be demons.

They're an unusual unit: Although they're technically part of the same army, they don't actually serve under the Demon Lord. This is also why the Ninth Army is the only formation that didn't participate in the big battle.

Anyway, the Tenth Army was still without a commander, and I was without an official job title, so here we are.

But at this point, most of the available personnel had already been assigned elsewhere…

So the Tenth Army mostly wound up with little fledglings fresh out of the academy, people who couldn't stay in other armies for various reasons, and so on.

Basically, nobody all that great.

The Eighth Army was already a collection of disposable pawns, but these people didn't even fit in there.

But when you look at each of their histories, it's actually pretty entertaining.

Especially my sub-commander, Phelmina.

Most of this girl's life is a serious sob story, the kind you can't even talk about without crying.

And it's basically all Vampy's fault!

Phelmina is a young lady from an important noble family.

She was even engaged to a similarly noble young man. Typical aristocracy stuff.

As such, she was raised from infancy to be a future leader of the demon race, undergoing all kinds of severe training. She was already talented to begin with, which meant her life was going smoothly until she entered the academy.

But that's where it all hit the fan.

When she got to the academy, she met a suspicious young woman from who-knows-where.

You guessed it: Vampy.

A wild child who couldn't care less about noble etiquette, she wreaked havoc at the academy in more ways than one.

Technically, Vampy is a noblewoman from an important family, too, but her home and family got destroyed when she was a baby, so she's been a vagrant child ever since…

Not that it matters, since being from a human noble family doesn't teach you anything about demon noble etiquette anyway.

Demons are more concerned with combat ability.

In that respect, Vampy got super strong in terms of stats and skills on our journey, and apparently, that seriously hurt the pride of her classmates.

Now, if that was all she did, it wouldn't be so bad.

Squashing the pride of some little demon kids? Who cares?

If that was enough to keep them down forever, then they were never destined for greatness in the first place.

But that was nothing compared to the chaos she caused next.

What did Vampy do, exactly? Well, she used her vampire abilities to Charm all the boys into bending to her will and drank a bunch of their blood to boot.

…Yeah, I know. A lot to take in, right?

I mean, I guess that might be what vampires are supposed to do, but yikes…

Apparently, when vampires enter puberty, their thirst for blood gets a lot stronger.

For vampires, drinking blood not only feeds them but also increases their number of underlings.

So yeah, it's like, y'know.

It sorta sounds like a certain sketchy kind of harassment, but I guess you could say they're around the age where they take an interest in that kind of thing, right?

You know how it is!

Most people would be able to control themselves, but apparently Vampy was extra stressed for various reasons, and she just kinda went wild.

She Charmed all the boys and basically became the empress of the academy.

It was Phelmina who rose up against her.

Phelmina's fiancé, Wald, was among the boys under Vampy's control, and the whole ruling class of the demons was in danger, so she took it upon herself to get rid of Vampy.

Obviously, she failed.

Vampy's legion of young men conspired against her, with Wald at the center.

They made full use of their family influence to put pressure on Phelmina's parents and got them to banish her instead.

Incidentally, Phelmina's family was a pretty important name among the demon nobles, too, but with similarly important families like Wald's and others turning against them, they had no choice but to exile Phelmina.

And she got screwed over like this all because Vampy has connections to the Demon Lord.

If anything had happened to Vampy, there was no telling what the Demon Lord might do. Thus, even the adults who were free to choose all decided to side against Phelmina.

I, uh, I'm sorry about my crew...

Thanks to my friends, Phelmina got chased out of demon society.

I would've felt kinda bad leaving her in the lurch.

Coincidentally enough, the former commander of the Tenth Army that I took over was Phelmina's father, so I ended up taking her under my command.

I mean, her handsome yet somehow unlucky-looking father begged me on hands and knees to take care of his daughter. What was I supposed to do?

Most members of the upper echelon of demon society sure seem to suffer a lot...

Although that's mostly the Demon Lord's fault!

...Seriously, I'm really sorry about my crew.

After that whole mess, Phelmina ended up being the first to join the Tenth Army.

Then other people in similarly bad situations joined, too, and the army started to take form.

Of course, the fact that all the members are here for messy reasons means they're all problem children.

So what do you think is the fastest way to deal with that?

That's right. The answer is give 'em a good thrashing until they obey you.

It's important to get the upper hand early.

Once you drill it into their heads that you're way stronger than them, they'll usually do whatever you say.

Hmm? It's barbaric to force them to obey me with brute strength?

I shouldn't break them in like animals, you say?

Well, people are animals, too, in the grand scheme of things!

Besides, saying stuff like that will get some animal welfare groups after me next, right?

Yeah, yeah.

But this is a parallel world!

There's no such thing as animal welfare groups here!

If there was any, maybe they should've protected me when I was a baby spider, dammit!

…Okay, we got a little off topic there.

So anyway, I use my overwhelming strength to make my new recruits listen to me, but there were still several problems.

One, we barely had any personnel. Two, they were weak. Three, no equipment.

There's not much I could do about that first one. This army is already made up of the dregs of the dregs in the first place.

It's inevitable that we wouldn't have a high head count.

But the second and third problems were serious.

Well, technically they were only weak by my personal standards. They weren't particularly weaker than other demon soldiers or anything.

But like I said, the Tenth Army doesn't have many members.

What we lack in numbers, we have to make up for with individual strength.

We're talking quality over quantity here.

As in, since I couldn't get a higher quantity, I had no choice but to shoot for a higher quality.

And because the Tenth Army was formed last and barely has any people, we hardly get any supplies like armor and weapons.

Everything gets distributed to the other armies first, leaving next to nothing for the Tenth.

As a result, my guys get stuck fighting with cloth armor and tree branches, like the starter equipment in some game.

That only makes it even more important that each individual member of the Tenth Army is strong enough to make up for their crummy equipment.

Add it all up, and I had no choice but to train them!

So that's exactly what I did.

Basically, I used the same approach you saw with Vampy and company: having them clean up some monsters and reaping energy for the system while we're at it.

Ah, but I didn't send them after legendary-class monsters or anything crazy like that, okay?

We started with the weaker monsters and worked our way up from there, of course.

I gauged the members' strength and picked difficulty levels just low enough that they wouldn't die.

Usually, I teleported all of them into the middle of a monster swarm, then teleported them home to rest once they were done.

Using my teleportation, I can send them to anywhere in the human and demon realms.

That makes it easy to visit monster-filled regions that neither demons nor humans would ever normally enter.

So I kept using my free army delivery service to drop my soldiers into the midst of monster hordes and bring them back, repeating the process to quickly level them up.

Thanks to that foolproof system, their levels went up really quickly, and they got stronger.

Then, once they had a certain level of basic strength, I subjected them to my personal training program.

In Vampy's case, I had her train and then level up, but we had more time back then.

Training before leveling is really more efficient, but we didn't have the luxury.

In order to make them as strong as possible in a limited time, the fastest method was to level them up quickly and get their stats to a point where they could keep up with the training.

If their stats were too low, my training regimen would just kill them.

Hmm? You can't really call it training if it might kill you?

Well, yeah, why do you think I threw them into swarms of monsters first?

What? Normally that would be considered a death sentence?

…Well, common sense is for losers!

Even if all my soldiers look like their souls left them, what's important is that they survived, leveled up, and made it back in one piece!

Nobody needs to know that I messed up my difficulty calculations a few times and almost got them killed.

Shh, it's fiiine.

That just taught them how to run and hide from opponents they can't defeat!

And here you see the results of that intensive training.

The huge horde of monkeys that was living in this fort has been completely wiped out.

Bravo! *Clap, clap, clap.*

"All clear."

I nod at Phelmina's report.

Excellent. That was great work.

Bwa-ha-ha! My Tenth Army has truly become a force to be reckoned with!

Incidentally, I solved our equipment shortage by going out of pocket.

Like I mentioned before, I weaved their white clothing with my own thread.

And I talked Mr. Oni into making weapons for them.

With his skill that lets him craft magic weapons, of course.

Thanks to him, the Tenth Army's soldiers are actually better equipped than everyone else now.

Unlike the rest of the demon army, they don't make a lot of public appearances; most of the Tenth's activities so far have been for training, and a lot of the rest has been for my personal goals.

Which is why people apparently think the Tenth Army is some kind of secret information-gathering task force or something.

Hrm. Well, I guess I have made them do stuff like that.

Mostly related to the elves. I've had them track down elves who are still mucking about in demon lands and dispose of them if they find any.

As far as that goes, a lot of it was taken care of before the big war broke out thanks to the Colonel, also known as the late First Army Commander Agner, so there wasn't much left for the Tenth Army to do anyway.

Which is why I sorta got carried away and sent them to hunt down elves in the human realm, too.

The only good elf is a dead elf, after all.

I used my teleportation to send my troops behind enemy lines, where they relied on their honed skills to conceal themselves, gather information, and assassinate any elves they found.

So yeah, I guess it's true they've done some covert mission stuff before.

Phelmina in particular seems to have a gift for that kind of thing. She's become an expert at sneaking up soundlessly behind a target and assassinating them without ever being noticed.

Since she's been here since the birth of the new Tenth Army, she's been trained longer than anyone else, and it definitely shows.

To be honest, she's probably stronger than the likes of Commander Boobs.

Phelmina would probably win in a head-to-head fight, and if there's no holds barred, I bet she could win even faster by killing someone in their sleep or something.

A young noblewoman turned assassin.

Yep, that's pretty damn cool!

Phelmina also gives orders to the troops for me, deals with paperwork and other administrative stuff, and just generally takes care of communications in my place, since I'm so bad at talking.

Thanks to her strict upbringing as a proper lady, she's great at all kinds of things.

At this point, she's essential to the Tenth Army!

Which is why she was unanimously chosen as the sub-commander.

Ah, the only one who objected to that was Vampy, but I shut her up by making her kneel.

As punishment to Vampy for getting Phelmina banished and all that, I put a little curse on her.

When I say *sit!* she has to get down on her hands and knees.

It's super handy whenever I need to punish Vampy for screwing up something or other.

And whenever Phelmina sees me force Vampy to kneel, it seems to cheer her up a bit, so that's a nice little bonus.

Since the rest of the members of the Tenth Army all know what Vampy did to Phelmina, too, they're always glaring daggers at our little bloodsucker.

The fact that Vampy doesn't get discouraged or even seem to notice it is kind of impressive.

She's got some serious guts, that one.

Meanwhile, Phelmina's ex-fiancé Wald always has a stomachache or some nonsense.

He's the one who got Charmed by Vampy in the academy and chased out Phelmina.

Now, that's not his fault, since he was Charmed. He's just a victim there.

But listen to this.

Even though the Charm effects wore off, he's still pining for Vampy. He joined the Tenth Army just to chase after her, and he even talked her into making him a vampire.

He's like an obsessive fan chasing Vampy around at this point.

And of course, the other Tenth Army members don't exactly look kindly on that...

Not to mention that his ex-fiancée Phelmina, whose life he basically ruined, is now his superior...

So it's not exactly a comfortable situation for Wald.

I swear, he looks paler every day. Oh, but that might be because he's a vampire now, I guess.

Anyway, as I reflect on all this, I go around collecting the dead monkeys scattered in the fortress.

Demons aren't going to eat monkeys, so somebody's gotta do it.

That means me, or more specifically, my little clones.

I keep tossing the monkey corpses into the pocket dimension where I keep my mini-mes, cleaning up the fortress.

Not that we're gonna use this fort anymore...

Because the Tenth Army is few in number, we can't really hold and maintain a fort like this as our base. We're just gonna leave it when our business is done here.

It'd be a waste to leave valuable manpower here. We might as well just give up on it and let some other demons use it for something more productive.

It's not like the humans are gonna come try to take it back anyway.

How can I be so sure, you ask?

Because I've set things up to make it happen that way.

Heh-heh-heh.

Do you really think I've been sitting around doing nothing for these past few years?

Truth be told, the mastermind who's manipulated the movements of not just the demon army, but even the humans, is none other than meeee!

DUN, DUN, DUNNN!

Man, it was a pain in the ass, I gotta say.

I had to teleport like crazy all over the place.

There were some serious machinations involved.

That big war between the demons and humans was one of the results of my hard work, see.

It took a ton of effort to get there, though.

I'm a very hard worker, if I do say so myself!

…But the hard work is still just getting started, as much as I hate to say it.

I'd better finish collecting these monkey corpses, reassemble the Tenth Army, and return to the Demon Lord's castle, stat.

I'll need my highly trained soldiers to help me out with the upcoming behind-the-scenes work. We can't be wasting time in some stupid monkey fortress.

The war was definitely a huge event, but when you look at the endgame the Demon Lord and I are aiming for, it was just one step of many along the way.

There's definitely no time to waste.

Not if we're going to save this world from certain destruction.

So as part of the groundwork for that goal, I'm going to give the Tenth Army a highly important, top-secret mission.

Specifically, I'm sending them to the Analeit Kingdom, home of our buddy Yamada and his big brother Julius the hero, to destroy the place from the inside.

2   Dealing with the Hero for a Living

The Analeit Kingdom.

It's a human nation on the continent of Daztrudia, separate from the continent Kasanagara, which is where you can find the demon realm.

But the royal authority in the Analeit Kingdom isn't particularly strong; it's more like the king leads together with the highest-ranking nobles.

Okay, I guess the political structure doesn't really matter.

There are two important points about this kingdom.

The fact that they have an academy where kids from all over the world gather, and the fact that it's peaceful there.

Well, I guess you could say the academy exists there *because* it's so peaceful.

Daztrudia doesn't have a demon nation, so the human-demon war isn't a big deal there. Instead, they have the Holy Kingdom of Alleius, which is the headquarters of the Word of God religion, and the other territories are all connected from there.

There aren't any big battles between nations and not many territories where nasty monsters exist, either.

Analeit Kingdom has a particularly stable climate and fertile land. Basically, they're super blessed.

Honestly, it'd be harder to *not* be prosperous and peaceful in their shoes.

No wonder it's an important kingdom. They're a bunch of cheaters!

Anyway, I'm guessing that super-stability is why they've started putting lots of effort into raising the next generation tender love and care, complete with a big academy.

At first, it was only for the noble kids within the kingdom, but somewhere along the way, it started to enroll students from all over the world.

I'm sure you can gather from that natural growth just how successful the kingdom is.

Although the fact that students have come from the other continent might be an effort to evacuate them from the front lines of battle.

After all, Kasanagara is the place where humans are suuuper at war with demons right now.

It makes sense that rich people would send their kids to the academy for safety.

So, since they're taking care of kids for nobles and sometimes even royalty from other nations, the Analeit Kingdom gets a nice fat connection with all those places.

That makes this academy *the* place to be.

And if you don't send your kids there, you'll be left out.

Sending your kids to the Analeit Kingdom academy has become a big status symbol and eventually turned into the norm for the upper class of noble society.

This has only made it even more important to stay connected.

Basically, it's a big cycle in the Analeit Kingdom's favor.

It's no exaggeration to say that they're second in influence only to the Word of God church.

They might even give the Church a run for their money.

Of course, it's typical of the Word of God that instead of trying to crush them, they started proactively trying to bring the Analeit Kingdom into their fold instead.

The Word of God has an established presence in the Analeit Kingdom, which means it also naturally reaches the kids who are studying abroad at their academy.

Man, that pontiff hasn't been guiding the human race all this time for nothing.

He's got a knack for naturally brainwashing people. Scary stuff…

So yeah, technically, the Analeit Kingdom is being used a bit, but they're still impressive.

They're even comparable to the Renxandt Empire, who are always battling it out with the demon realms on their border.

If the Renxandt Empire is the bulwark that protects humanity from the threat of demons, Analeit Kingdom is the safe zone far removed from the front lines.

As long as nothing totally insane happens, it's a place where humanity could take refuge.

That also means that if anything went wrong there, it would seriously freak out everyone around them.

Which is why we went to work in the Analeit Kingdom!

…At least, that's the official story.

Honestly, the amount of influence the Analeit Kingdom has on humanity doesn't actually matter that much to me, y'know?

I only have one reason for messing with them.

Because that's where Yamada is.

It's just…like…argh!

What the heck?!

Gahhh! Come onnn!

Aargh! Ugggh! Aaargh!

Whew.

Okay, that's enough yelling for no reason.

This is all because the stuff I've done backfired in ways I never imagined.

All my preparations were going so well, but then everything went ridiculously wrong somehow.

And all of that converged right on our pal Yamada.

In this world, his name is Schlain Zagan Analeit, also known as Shun.

The fourth prince of the Analeit Kingdom.

And he's the biological brother of the previous hero, Julius.

A prince of a major nation? The hero's little brother?

As if all that backstory wasn't overkill enough, then the craziest thing happened.

He became the new hero…

Do you have any idea how I felt when I found that out through my mini-me?

After I worked sooo hard to get rid of that hero!

The next one just *had* to be a reincarnation!

And on top of that, it's someone who had a deep connection with the previous hero!

This is awful! No, it's worse than awful!

How was I supposed to know this would happen?!

I've gotta readjust my plans—fast!

First of all, it goes without saying that our goal is to save this world from destruction.

Yeah, this world is doomed to be destroyed soon. That much is certain.

If nothing is done, it's a guaranteed game over.

So in order to avoid that, we're gonna destroy the system, which is basically this world's life support!

Bad idea? That'll just kill us off faster? Shh, don't think about that.

The system does keep this world alive, but it also contains an insane amount of energy.

And the whole reason this world is falling apart is that it doesn't have enough energy.

So our plan is to plunder all the energy the world needs from the system.

It's kinda like using the electricity that runs a life support system to deliver an electric shock directly to the patient and revive them.

I know it sounds pretty risky, but it should work in theory.

Not to mention, it was that crafty Administrator D who set up the system in the first place, so I had a feeling there would be a backdoor method to do something like that.

I took a look, and sure enough, it really did exist...

Anyway, we're carrying out our break-the-system plan, which means we have to make some arrangements first.

Like I said before, this system-breaking plan is a huge risk.

If it fails, this world is gonna collapse on the spot without its life-support system.

Which is why we've got to take every possible precaution to make sure nothing goes wrong.

You could even say that everything I've done these past few years has been for that purpose.

Honestly, the huge war between demons and humans was just one small part of our bigger plan.

There were two main goals.

One: to secure more energy.

It requires energy to destroy the system, and we didn't have enough.

The only way to get the energy we needed was a huge amount of deaths.

This is because the system works by absorbing the stats and skills people improve during their lifetimes in the form of energy when they die.

Just as we hoped, we were able to gain the bare minimum amount of energy we need from all the casualties after war broke out.

But it's still just the bare minimum. Ideally, we'd like to have extra just in case something unexpected happens.

It's only thanks to the noble sacrifices of many demons and humans that we succeeded in securing the necessary energy at all.

Yeah, it's awful for the people who got turned into energy, but this is to save the world from destruction.

The needs of the many outweigh the needs of the few and all that.

Just ignore the fact that the "few" in this case is an insanely huge number.

All that matters is that without that huge amount of sacrifices, this world would be screwed to the point of no return.

So. Anyway.

The most important of those many valuable sacrifices was the hero.

That was our second major goal: obliterating the hero!

See, the hero is a huge cheater by nature.

It's like an official cheat code that was built into the system...

You get all kinds of benefits just for being the hero, but the scariest of those is the anti-demon-lord effect.

The demon lord is chosen from among the demons, but demons live way longer and have way higher stats than humans.

Which means humanity could never defeat an experienced demon lord.

To make up for that, the hero is designed to be super effective against the demon lord.

No matter how strong the demon lord might be, the hero will always have the ability to be more than a match for them.

...With backup from the system.

...Consuming a corresponding amount of energy.

And who is the demon lord right now?

Yes, it's the Origin Taratect you all know and love, Ms. Ariel herself!

She's by far the strongest individual in the world! I mean, stats averaging around 90,000? Is that a bug or a typo or something?

So what would happen if the demon lord clashed with the hero?

If the system provided the hero with backup to beat her, you better believe it would waste a massive amount of energy.

Obviously, we don't want our Demon Lord to get killed, of course, but either way, that means we can't allow the hero to fight the demon lord no matter what.

To make matters worse, the hero even has a special weapon.

It's called the Sword of the Hero.

Hilariously cliché, I know, but its ability is no joke.

It only works once, but it can kill anyone in a single blow, even a god.

…That means even I would die if it hit me, right?

D is the one who made it, after all.

So, like, I'm just thinking out loud here, but it's probably supposed to be another sneaky trick, like "You can use this to kill Güli-güli and get tons of energy if you want."

Just like breaking the system itself…

Or maybe it's for if some random foreign god came wandering into this world or something?

Either way, that Sword of the Hero spells doom for anyone, even me.

Just letting that thing continue to exist is dangerous!

So our other goal was to get rid of it, obviously.

Ideally by making the hero die after wasting it on something!

One problem, though! If we kill the hero, a new one's just gonna pop up anyway!

So I tried to mess with the system itself and erase the very existence of heroes!

By erasing the settings for heroes from the system, basically.

So the plan was to kill Julius the hero, then hack the system before the title moved on to the next one.

It was practically a frame-perfect trick, but I did plenty of preparation beforehand, so it was no problem.

…At least, it wasn't *supposed* to be.

Well, to get right to the point, that obviously didn't work out.

And after I worked so hard to set everything up...

We made a queen taratect clone like Mother and sent it after him, thinking he'd have to use the Sword of the Hero to beat it, but he won without using it...

I even had to show up personally...

Considering that the hero's special cheat ability might've activated even against me, I was hoping he'd naturally get killed by someone else, y'know?

In retrospect, his cheat code might have helped him beat the queen taratect clone in the first place.

The Colonel and Deadbeat both went down in the fight against the hero party, too.

I was planning on bringing them back whenever I could find an opening, but they had to go and act all manly and cool...

...We did succeed in defeating the hero, but honestly, the overall plan was a failure.

A *major* failure.

A really, really unbelievably major failure!

...*Sigh.*

Well, in a way, it stands to reason that my calculations went wrong.

We were trying to get Julius the hero killed for our cause and it's only natural that he fought back.

Obviously, Julius didn't know the real story. All he did was fight like a hero should.

He fought fair and square and totally shattered our expectations in the process.

I was taking the hero way too lightly.

I mean, I *thought* I was being careful. That's why I made all kinds of preparations and formed a whole plan just to kill him.

But what I was really being wary of was the "Hero" as a function of the system.

Not Julius, the individual.

That was my mistake.

Now I know that what I really should have feared is the fact that he was chosen to be the hero.

After all, the title is only given to the most fitting person for the job. A mere human who would be the best receptacle for the miraculous power of the hero.

He's not strong because of his cheat code powers. He's strong because he was a worthy individual who could be entrusted with those powers.

Faith, determination, pride.

Those powers of the heart are what really make a hero formidable.

So really, I was probably bound to fail from the moment I made that miscalculation.

I accept that part as my mistake.

But that being said, I have a few complaints about what happened next!

I mean, seriously?! The next hero turned out to be YAMADA?!

Honestly, for the most part, it wouldn't matter which human became the hero.

After all, most important humans participated in the big war, and over half of them died. Plus the half that's left aren't really worth much in comparison to Julius the hero.

Even if it went to a promising youngster who didn't participate in the war, well, a young kid becoming the hero would be even more advantageous for us.

Such a young hero would never grow up in time to factor into our plans.

No matter how broken the hero's official cheat powers might be, they're not all powerful—I proved that when I defeated Julius.

Even if someone a bit inconvenient for us became the Hero, worst-case scenario, I could just take care of 'em nice and quick.

Or so I thought!

But the worst-case scenario turned out to be even worse than I thought.

It was none other than Yamada, who's hard enough to lay a hand on as a reincarnation and one of the strongest to boot.

Well, let's put aside the power level conversation for a second.

Considering the full strength of our forces, it doesn't really matter who the hero is; they won't be a threat to us.

The strongest reincarnation would probably be either Kushitani or Tagawa, followed by Yamada.

Kushitani and Tagawa have been traveling around as adventurers, building up experience.

And even that pair together weren't able to defeat Mera on his own.

You couldn't even take Mera, huh...?

Heh-heh. He's actually the weakest of us...

If you can't even beat him, you reincarnations should be ashamed...

Okay, that was just an Elite Four bit, but Mera really is the weakest of us.

If the two strongest reincarnations can't even beat him, then we've got nothing to worry about in terms of strength.

Now that Yamada's become the hero, it's likely he's surpassed those two in terms of stats, but it probably evens out since he's got practically no hands-on combat experience, don't you think?

So their strength doesn't really matter, but that's not the part we need to worry about.

First of all, Yamada is a reincarnation.

That makes it hard for me to lay a hand on him.

Okay, so personally, I don't really care that much either way, but Ms. Oka has been trying sooo hard to save all the reincarnations. I don't wanna ruin that for her.

I owe Ms. Oka a lot.

This was in our past lives, but she did save my life.

I want to pay her back for that.

So I'm trying to respect her wishes as much as possible, meaning I try to save reincarnations whenever I can.

Which means the fastest solution—killing the new hero—isn't an ideal option here.

Not to mention, Yamada himself is raring to follow in Julius's footsteps.

He wants to avenge the hero, who was also his big brother.

If he's that fired up about it, he's bound to get in our way when we try to make a move.

After all, we are the demon army.

More specifically, I am the one who personally killed Julius…

And finally, this part is the hardest to predict and the most annoying: Yamada's unique skill.

By using my mini-mes to gather information, I found out that his unique skill as a reincarnation is called Divine Protection.

The effect is that it apparently makes the results he wants more likely to happen…

Talk about an abstract description.

I mean, it's basically just a luck-based thing.

Most skills have their effects described in concrete, predefined numbers, but it's totally impossible to figure out the extent of this one's effects.

Even if things go well for him, there's no way of telling whether that was thanks to his own abilities, good luck, or the help of this stupid Divine Protection skill.

But that's the skill that worries me the most.

The unique skills D gave specially to each reincarnation aren't usually so vague.

It might normally be little more than a slight boost in luck that you wouldn't even notice, but I'm guessing that when it comes down to a really crucial moment, it means he'll never make the wrong decision.

But that depends on Yamada himself.

In other words, it might bring about the worst possible results for someone he considers an enemy.

And obviously, that enemy has got to be us...

If worse comes to worst, a choice that Yamada thinks is right might even end up preventing our goal of saving the world from destruction. It's crazy, but it could happen.

Since the effect is so hard to understand, there's no telling how much this Divine Protection skill could intervene with what you might call fate itself, and that's what's so scary about it.

And so hard to plan for.

So, with all that in mind, I'm planning to take Yamada out of the picture for a bit.

Oh, I don't mean send him to the afterworld or anything terrible like that, of course!

I'm just trying to physically distance him from the situation so he can't interfere.

Since we were able to get rid of Julius the hero, clearly Yamada's Divine Protection isn't all-powerful.

Otherwise, it wouldn't have let the person Yamada cared about so much die.

So I'm guessing that Divine Protection can't prevent something that's happening outside of Yamada's awareness, probably. Hopefully.

So we're just gonna destroy the Analeit Kingdom real quick.

Huh? That still sounds pretty terrible?

Shh. Don't even worry about it.

All right, let's go take down a monarchy, people!

V1 Working for the Mastermind

"Heh-heh-heh. Finally. I can finally pay those bastards back for what they did to me!"

Oh, dear me.

Someone thinks he's cool...

"Hey, Sophia! Don't just stand there! Let's go!"

"Coming, coming."

A man decked out in full armor yells at me impatiently as I roll my eyes.

Normally, I wouldn't stand for this kind of treatment for a second, but it's hard to get angry when I think about how pathetic this loser is.

The man stomping around in front of me with his shoulders squared is Hugo Baint Renxandt.

He's the prince of the Renxandt Empire and a student here at the Analeit Kingdom academy.

Not that he actually goes to school all that much.

Apparently, he screwed the pooch about five years ago and got suspended.

I don't know what he screwed up exactly, because I didn't care enough to ask. Judging by his ranting about "those bastards," though, I'm guessing he messed with the wrong crowd and had the tables turned on him somehow?

Then I suppose one of "those bastards" is probably Schlain, the prince of this kingdom, who's our current target.

Oh brother.

What in the world am I doing here anyway?

This "pulling the strings" business? Is that what you'd call it?

Either way, it really isn't my thing.

I'd much prefer to just punch the problem square in the face and be done with it.

But I just have to keep telling myself that all this is necessary.

Supporting this idiot Hugo is the role I've been given.

He's a reincarnation, too, but I'm really only helping him because Master decided his grudge would make him a convenient pawn to for our purposes.

…When I think about it that way, it really is pitiful.

And I can still remember the moment he was set up as a pawn with perfect clarity.

"Shit! I won't let it end like this! This is my world! It exists for me, only for me! Like I'd accept this ending?! Not a chance in hell! It's not over until everything belongs to me!"

"Damn that elf! I'll have my revenge! She's gonna rue the day she messed with me!"

"I'll take away everything she has someday! Just like she did to me!"

"Just you wait! I'll destroy everything she holds dear! Then I'll beat her to a pulp while she screams and cries over their remains!"

"You watch! I'm gonna take this world back for myself!"

Hugo was screaming and throwing a fit.

"Shall I help you out with that?"

Since he completely failed to notice me, I got bored and addressed him myself.

"Who's there?!"

Hugo whirled around.

Master teleported me directly into Hugo's room, so from his point of view, it was like I suddenly appeared directly behind him.

I couldn't blame him for being surprised.

This was the perfect chance to teach the panicking little fool that I was above him.

"I'd be willing to lend you a hand, since we're fellow reincarnations and all, hmm?"

I put on a meaningful, unconcerned smile.

"…Huh? Reincarnation?"

Hugo's brow furrowed.

Well, I suppose he wasn't stupid enough to jump at the chance to work with some suspicious stranger who randomly appeared in his…

"…Whatever. I don't care who the hell you are. If I can get revenge on those bastards, I'll even work with a demon or whatever else!"

Ah, he *is* stupid enough.

"Hell yeah. I'm in!"

"There you have it. What do you think, Master?"

"Hunh?"

A white shadow flitted behind Hugo's back.

The figure covered Hugo's mouth with one hand, preventing him from screaming.

Then, once he could no longer move, the other hand lightly touched Hugo's forehead.

And a tiny white spider small enough to fit on your fingertip crawled down the hand and into Hugo's ear…

Seconds later, Hugo's body started convulsing.

Just like that, his eyes rolled back and he passed out.

Yes, it's quite a disgusting story all right…

Even now, as he saunters along brimming with confidence, that little spider is in his head…

Hugo doesn't seem to remember that incident, but ever since then, he's been strangely obedient whenever I tell him to do something.

So that spider must be brainwashing him…

Could there be one of those in my head, too…?

I quickly shake my head to chase out the awful thought.

She did put a weird curse on me, but she would never go so far as to put a spider in my head!

…Probably.

…No, she wouldn't.

Master will cut down anything in her path without mercy, but she's actually quite soft on the people she cares about.

Since that technically includes me, I'm sure she wouldn't do something like that.

Although she does have somewhat different moral standards than most people, which means she sometimes does the most disturbing things without batting an eye.

Seriously, who starts an entire war just to accomplish their goals?

Especially one so huge that both the human and demon sides suffered massive losses.

But the fact she would do that without a moment's hesitation is what makes her my master, I suppose.

And yet, she's incredibly overprotective when it comes to her inner circle.

That much is obvious from her attitude toward Ms. Ariel.

Ms. Ariel is quite a bit stronger than me, but Master really shelters her so carefully, making sure to keep her away from the battlefield and any even the remote possibility of danger.

Honestly, I'm a bit jealous.

Something stirs in my chest, but I rein it in through sheer force of will.

That was too close.

Envy almost got out of control there.

The Envy skill I have is highly effective, but it also has serious drawbacks.

It makes it much harder to control my emotions.

My feelings have always been on the intense side, but the Envy skill has made them that much more extreme.

I know I have a bad habit of acting on my emotions without thinking, and I would like to fix that, but it's easier said than done.

Though I have gained the Heresy Resistance skill to help reduce the effects of Envy.

But it hasn't become Heresy Nullification yet, so it still can't completely cancel out the effects.

I have to control myself.

Careful to avoid being noticed, I take a few deep breaths to calm down.

Meanwhile, Hugo has already reached our destination ahead of me.

He slams the door open without so much as a knock.

"...You could at least knock."

"C'mon, we're pals, aren't we? Deal with it."

The man waiting in the room greets Hugo with a deepening furrow in his brow.

This is the first prince Cylis, who appears to be in a bad mood twenty-four seven.

Like Hugo, he's one of our pawns.

Pawn Number Two, you might call him.

He's a dull, pathetic man with nothing of note about him except his pride and the fact that he can't admit that his younger brothers are superior to him.

He's the first prince and son of the true queen, yet the second prince Julius was far more famous than him, being the hero and all.

And Julius's full brother, the fourth prince Schlain, has been a child prodigy all his life.

Meanwhile, the future king Cylis is average at best.

So he's afraid that one of his younger brothers is going to steal the throne from him, you see.

When we offered to help him chase out his younger brother, he took the bait right away.

Basically, it's the kind of power struggle you see all the time in legends and such.

"This *is* going to work, right?"

Cylis puts on a pompous tone to hide his fearfulness.

"Of course it is," snaps Hugo. "Who the hell do you think I am?"

Honestly. He has a lot of nerve for someone who's borrowing other people's power to try and grab the throne instead of relying on himself.

What a pathetic little man.

Although it's that nature that allows us to use him so easily.

"And no one saw your face?"

"Duh! Look at what I'm wearing!"

Hugo holds up his arms and turns in a circle to show off his armor.

He's currently decked out in full-body armor and wearing a helmet that covers his face.

Nobody will be able to tell who's inside.

That much should be obvious at a glance; this so-called prince must be seriously worried to ask such a stupid question.

There's nothing to worry about, you fool.

Don't you know who's backing you up?

Failure is simply not in the realm of possibility.

Ahh, although I suppose technically…that's as far as *our* goals are concerned, not necessarily these two.

Cylis paces around the room anxiously.

On the other hand, Hugo flops down in a chair, looking unconcerned.

I lean against the wall with my arms folded, waiting.

It should be any moment now.

Listening carefully, I hear someone knock on the door of the next room over.

"It's Schlain."

"Hmm? Come in."

"Thank you."

Ah, so it's begun.

Our target, Schlain, has entered the room next to us.

"What is it?"

That voice belongs to the owner of the room Schlain has entered: his and Cylis's father, the king of this kingdom.

"You're the one who called for us, aren't you, Father? What is it you need?"

"Hmm? I didn't call for you."

Well, of course you didn't.

After all, we're the ones who summoned him here.

After that, things fall unnaturally silent.

In sharp opposition to that silence, I sense magic filling the room next door.

They're using Wind Magic to muffle the sound.

And then the caster speaks.

"Aaaaaah! Brother! What are you doing?!"

Pfft.

What an awful actress.

The girl who just delivered that very forced cry is the one who cast the spell.

With that scream as his signal, Cylis runs out of the room, throws the other door open, and charges inside.

Hugo follows behind him.

I walk unhurriedly after the two.

"What's going on?!"

"Brother Schlain attacked Father!"

"He did what?! Schlain, have you gone mad?!"

Oh? From the sound of things, Cylis actually isn't half bad at acting.

Maybe he should go into theater instead of seeking the throne?

Well, I guess it's a little late for that.

"Guards! Schlain has attacked His Majesty!"

Cylis's voice echoes clearly through the hallway.

That's actually because I've increased its volume with magic.

This way, even people who don't know anything about what's going on should be able to hear him.

"Seize him!"

As I casually peer into the room from the hallway, Hugo is just slashing at Schlain with his sword.

The room is in quite a sorry state.

The king has been shot through the forehead and killed, Schlain is clutching his just-opened wound, and a small young woman is standing there expressionless.

"Yo. You don't look so good, Mr. Hero."

"You...Hugo...?"

"That's right."

Hugo takes off his helmet.

"Hugo. Don't go giving yourself away like that."

"C'mon, why not? I wanted him to get a good look at me before he dies."

Schlain looks utterly confused by the exchange between Cylis and Hugo.

As such, he doesn't even notice me entering the room.

"You're curious, right? See, your big brother here wants the throne. I want revenge on you and Oka. So you're a thorn in both our sides, get it?"

"But...why...? Cylis is already next in line for the throne..."

"Funny you should mention that. See, before he kicked the bucket, that stupid king was planning to make you his heir. He figured if you were declared as the next king before you could be declared as the hero, they wouldn't wanna send you into battle!"

"As if I would let my throne be stolen away for such a foolish reason!"

It's true that the king was planning to make Schlain the next king.

We didn't even have anything to do with that part.

Although the rest of it is mostly our fault.

"Brother. Unfortunately, you must now die here."

This line comes from Suresia, the princess of this kingdom, who's been silent all this time.

Since she's a princess, that means she's Schlain and Cylis's sister, of course.

"Sue, why?"

"I have opened my eyes to true love, dear brother. I would do anything for the sake of that love, even if I must kill my own brother."

This Suresia girl was apparently really attached to Schlain, so he must be extra surprised by this turn of events.

"Hugo! Is this your doing?!"

I suppose it makes sense he would figure that much out, then.

"Oh dear. You noticed, huh? Took you long enough. Yeah, I did it. What do you think? How's it feel to have something stolen from you? Sucks, right? I should know, since the same thing happened to me! Ga-ha-ha-ha!"

Hugo has a certain skill: Lust.

Like my Envy, it's from an especially powerful line of skills called the Seven Deadly Sins skills.

Its primary effect is brainwashing.

That's how he's controlling Suresia.

"Change her back right now!"

"You think I'm gonna do that just 'cause you asked nicely? What a moron."

For all the scorn Hugo is throwing at Schlain, he has no idea that the brainwasher is also being brainwashed himself.

How pathetic.

He's caught up in a temporary sense of superiority.

Although thanks to his arrogance, he's forgetting that a cornered rat bites back.

"Oof! How do you still have so much strength?!"

Schlain is so furious that he's thrown a punch at Hugo.

Looks like he's going to follow up with some Attack Magic, too.

I suppose I'd better help that idiot out.

"Oh? He's got more fight in him than I expected."

"?!"

I activate my Divine Scales and Dragon Barrier skills to prevent the casting of magic.

At the same time, I stop hiding my presence and allow my aura to fully permeate the room.

Immediately, Schlain rolls to the side to put distance between us.

Well, well. That's a half-decent reaction.

As I'm momentarily impressed, Schlain turns to look at me, and a strange sensation assails my body.

This feeling…Appraisal, I'm sure.

Tough luck for him, though.

As the holder of the Envy skill, I'm also a Ruler.

I can use my ruler authority to block Appraisal, you know.

So he won't be able to read my stats.

"Sophia! This one's mine! Don't go stickin' your nose where it don't belong!"

"Oh really? Looked like he was beating you up to me."

Idiot. He would've been in trouble if I hadn't helped out.

"Enough! Stop arguing and finish Schlain off quickly!"

…Would you mind not ordering me around?

Besides, I can't have anyone killing Schlain.

So we'll need our next player to show up and help him escape.

"I won't let you!"

There, see? Help has arrived.

A small-framed figure jumps into the room.

She unleashes some magic immediately, blowing Hugo away.

Although my Dragon Barrier skill reduces its power, so it doesn't deal much damage.

"Ooookaaaaa!!"

See? Look, he's perfectly fine.

But I should probably prevent her from attacking him any further.

This tiny intruder is the elf who was our teacher Ms. Oka in our previous lives. I cancel out her next magic spell with my own.

"Y-you?!"

Her eyes widen.

We did just run into each other recently, I suppose.

And it was a rather shocking scene, too.

No wonder she's surprised to see me here.

"Shun! Run for it!"

Ms. Oka uses magic to break the floor, scattering dust everywhere.

"But!"

"No buts! We have to withdraw for now!"

"Mr. Hyrince?"

"Leston told me you were in danger, so I came running. I'm sure you're confused, but we just have to get you out of here for now."

I hear this conversation amid the dust, followed by the sound of running footsteps.

"What are you doing?! After them!"

Cylis shouts, but Hugo and I both ignore him.

"Now, be sure to follow the plan, all right?"

"Yeah, you got it."

Hugo sneers and steps toward Cylis.

"...What is this?"

Sensing something is off, Cylis backs away.

"Oh, no big deal. Just gonna mess around in your head a little bit."

"Wha—?!"

Hugo's hand shoots out and clamps around Cylis's face.

"What are you doing?!"

"Changing our deal. You're gonna work as our disposable pawn from here on out."

"G-gahhhh?!"

Cylis screams in anguish.

I leave the room without waiting around to see it through to the end.

What Hugo is doing to Cylis right now isn't brainwashing—he's destroying his spirit.

Why not brainwash him? Because someone else is already doing it.

Cylis was being controlled from the start.

I doubt he was aware of it himself, and it wasn't total control, just nudging his thoughts in the right direction, or so I'm told.

But that controller can turn him into a completely mindless puppet, as long as they don't mind damaging his spirit like Hugo is doing right now.

And the only way to overwrite that control is to break his spirit completely.

Basically, we're erasing everything from his mind, including the other person's control.

The truth is, there are lots of other people in this kingdom who are already being secretly controlled just like Cylis.

The king was one of them.

That's why we killed him.

We needed to overthrow the Analeit Kingdom because its top brass were already victims of mind control.

Master even said that the decision to make Schlain the next king was probably the result of their thoughts being manipulated, too. We don't know for sure what the goal was, though.

According to Master, her best guess is that they wanted to keep Schlain the hero close by and accessible instead of handing him over to the Church.

We had to completely crush the kingdom in order to root out all the corruption.

Which is why we're currently doing some pest extermination in the castle.

We have Cylis's soldiers attacking the people we identified as being mind controlled.

And among those soldiers are members of the Tenth Army in disguise.

There's no way they won't accomplish their tasks.

Meanwhile, I'm on my way to destroy the mastermind who was trying to control this kingdom from the shadows.

"Good day to you."

I arrive in one of the guest rooms of the castle.

Waiting for me there is none other than Potimas.

"...I knew it. You lot are responsible for all this commotion, then."

"Pest control is a big undertaking, you know."

"Hmph. How irritating."

Potimas stands and faces me unhurriedly.

"...I cannot defeat you in this body."

"Oh? How very gracious of you."

This man can possess replicas of his body and control them from a distance, while his real self is still in the elf village.

So the real one won't die no matter how many bodies of his we kill.

That's probably why he's so calm, but I didn't expect him to give up without a fight.

"I have a message for White and Ariel." Potimas's expression doesn't change, but there's a dark flame burning deep in his eyes as he speaks. "I am waiting in the elf village. Come, and I will crush your conceited delusions with all my might."

"I'll be sure to let them know."

Although knowing Master, she's probably listening in through one of her clones already.

I can't stand looking at that unpleasant face of his for another second, so I promptly chop it off.

Potimas's head rolls across the floor.

Honestly, though, Master...

I can't believe he would put her name before Ariel, who's been his sworn enemy for so many years. He must have a serious grudge at this point.

Although I'm sure she's done enough to earn it.

Now, then.

As long as Schlain escapes safely, the plan will be a success.

But that wouldn't be very entertaining, would it?

I'm feeling a little dissatisfied, especially after Potimas didn't even fight back.

So...

Perhaps I'll go have a little fun.

SOPHIA KEREN

Sophia has a unique history: She was born in the human nation of Sariella and raised in the demon territory. She is now a fully-fledged vampire and the holder of the Seven Deadly Sins skill Envy. Between her history, species, and the effects of her skills, her wild actions inevitably stand out. After being repressed for much of her life, she now has a twisted personality and takes pleasure in the misfortune of others. Since she also has a tendency to act without thinking, there's no telling what trouble she might cause without White's control. Currently, she works under White's watchful eyes as part of the Tenth Army, serving both as a combatant and an undercover errand girl in various lands.

Conversation   THE ELF'S TRAGEDY

"Oh? It's been a while."

A young girl sweetly smiled at me.

The last time I saw her was years ago, when she was still a little girl.

She was so small, with nowhere to go—someone I thought I had to protect.

But by the time we met again…

"Shouko…Negishi…"

"Would you mind not calling me by that name?"

Negishi licked her fingertip, looking displeased.

The seductive gesture made her seem far more mature than her years.

It was as if to show me plainly that she's no longer a child, no longer in need of my protection.

All the more so because it was fresh blood she was licking off her finger.

"My policy is that our past lives are the past, and this is the present. I'm not the kind of person who needs her teacher's pity anymore."

"Pity? But I…"

I couldn't completely deny Negishi's words.

Her position in her past life couldn't be described as a good one by any stretch of the imagination.

She certainly didn't fit in with the class.

I did my best to reach out to her whenever I could, but if you asked whether that came out of my pride as a teacher or pity for her as a person, I have to admit I would be hard-pressed to answer.

"How...?! How can this be?!" the elf summoner shrieked.

The blood on Negishi's hand came from the monster he'd summoned.

He was one of the most famous and powerful elf summoners, and the beast he had called upon was one of the strongest.

Its danger level was S rank, a monster on par with wyrms and dragons, but it was swiftly ripped apart beyond all recognition.

"How?! How...?"

As the summoner repeated his cries deliriously, his voice was suddenly cut short.

I looked over to see his body collapsing, his head removed from the neck.

The chakram that must have beheaded him flew back into the hands of a white-clad girl, who had appeared seemingly from nowhere at Negishi's side.

As I stood there dumbfounded, all the other elves around me were gone.

Their bodies now on the ground.

A sea of blood began spreading around me.

"Why...would you...do this...?"

The question rose from my lips unbidden.

"Why? Because the elves are a nuisance to us."

Negishi answered as if it were obvious.

"Us?"

"Yes. Us."

"So you really are with the demons..."

The last time I saw Negishi was near the border of the empire.

After that, she was taken to the demon territory.

So I suspected that she must have ended up joining their side.

"The demons? Yes, I suppose that's one way to put it."

"What?"

But her response was strangely phrased.

"We are technically putting the demons to work. But I don't think it's quite accurate to lump us in with them."

"You're not with the demons...?"

Then what in the world is going on?

"You wouldn't know about the Administrators, would you?"

My eyes widened at that word.

How? Why?

The "Administrators" she refers to are unbelievable beings.

Even though I'd been taught about them all my life, I was never sure if they even really existed.

"I can't believe the elves are trying to oppose them. How stupid can you get?"

"It can't be! You mean you're doing this under the Administrators' orders?!"

"Isn't that what I just said?"

"Ms. Sophia."

As Negishi rolled her eyes and shrugged, the girl in the white clothes addressed her reproachfully.

"I know, I know. I've already said too much, right? You're such a stick-in-the-mud."

Negishi laughed at the other girl teasingly.

That smile made her almost look like a normal girl her age...

...save for the fact that she was standing in a sea of blood she had wrought herself.

I didn't understand how she could laugh so casually under such dire circumstances.

That was when I realized she wasn't the Negishi I knew anymore.

She was always a difficult child, but it felt like I was talking to a completely different beast, one who was far more terrifying.

"Well, then. I'll let you go this time, since you're an old acquaintance and all. Now that you see the difference in our strength, don't get in our way again."

Then, with a brisk wave, she led the white-clad group away.

This all happened not long ago.

I was in the empire, near demon lands, to investigate the ongoing disappearances of elves in the area.

Although I brought along the summoner and several other skilled elves, I was the only one who survived.

And that was only because I was spared, not because I was strong enough...

Which I'm sure was the case just now, too...

We fled to a mansion that Leston uses as his base.

"Leston is supposed to meet us here. Then we'll slip out of the country."

"Ms. Oka, wait! We have to do something about Hugo, or Sue will—!"

"We can't."

Shun wants to go back to fight Hugo and put a stop to this rebellion, but that's just not possible.

Not as long as Negishi is there!

Even if Shun is the hero now, I doubt he can win against someone who could effortlessly destroy an S-rank monster.

How did she get here, when she was in the far-off demon realm not long ago?

All I can think of is that Hugo let her use a teleport gate.

The kingdom and the empire each have a teleport gate, which allows one to warp across the long distance between them instantly.

The empire borders the demon realm, and I already know that Negishi was assassinating elves there anyway.

I don't know how, but she must have made contact with Hugo while she was undercover in the empire.

Then she zeroed in on Hugo's power and decided to use him...

At any rate, this situation couldn't be worse.

I don't know how far Sophia's side can reach with their power. We have to leave this kingdom and take refuge somewhere safe.

"But, Ms. Oka, if we can stop Hugo, this whole thing should blow over. We have to go back and catch him..."

"No."

"Ms. Oka!"

Even if I explain how dangerous Negishi is, I doubt Shun will accept it.

So I'll approach from a different angle.

"The Church has announced the new hero. His name is Hugo Baint Renxandt."

The Holy Kingdom of Alleius is the headquarters of the Word of God religion.

Just a few days ago, their pontiff presented the name of the next hero: Hugo.

That announcement is the reason I came hurrying back to this kingdom.

"Huh?"

Shun gapes at me blankly.

I had a similar reaction when I first heard this news.

Titles are absolute, and Shun is undoubtedly the holder of the hero title.

And yet, the Church pronounced Hugo the hero instead.

Clearly, something shady was in the works.

And sure enough, I arrived to find this disaster unfolding.

"Even the Church is working with him."

That's the only possible conclusion I could reach.

As I said before, titles are absolute.

The Appraisal skill is rare, but there are some people in the world who have it, like Shun himself.

And there's also the existence of Appraisal Stones.

The fact that Hugo isn't the hero would be found out immediately if either was used on him.

Since the Church put forth such a ridiculous claim nonetheless, they must have some hidden motive in mind.

"Do the elves have any idea why the Church would be complicit in such an absurd plot?"

Mr. Hyrince seems to have reached the same conclusion.

I've already come up with the answer.

"Most likely, it's safe to assume that Hugo's brainwashing has allowed him to worm his way into the Church."

Shun told me on the way here that Sue was being controlled by Hugo.

Following that logic, I concluded that Hugo must have used that power to take control over the Church and make them announce him as the new hero.

"Impossible. The effects of brainwashing are limited. It's not powerful enough to incite a situation like this, is it?"

Hyrince seems doubtful, but considering what Sue did, it's easy to see that's not the case.

It's incredibly difficult to brainwash someone enough to drive them to kill themselves or someone else.

Even back on Earth, it was said that using suggestion and such to make someone do something they strongly objected to would be all but impossible.

The same holds true in this world: Even if some skills can temporarily make someone obey the user, the brainwashing will quickly fail if the victim rejects it strongly enough.

But there is just one skill that makes all those things possible.

"Usually, no. But there is one exception."

"An exception?"

"One of the top-class Seven Deadly Sins series skills, Lust. Its brainwashing effect is far more powerful than any other skill can induce. I have no doubt that Hugo now holds this skill."

There is a limited amount of special skills in this world.

The Seven Deadly Sins series and the Seven Heavenly Virtues series.

I learned the basic information about these skills from Potimas, after asking for certain reasons.

And one of those skills is Lust.

It uses potent brainwashing to force the afflicted to obey the user.

All of the Seven Deadly Sins skills Potimas told me about had extraordinary effects, but Lust stuck out in my mind as especially horrid.

Still, Potimas was only guessing at the skill's effects from a person who once had the Lust skill in the past, so he didn't know exactly how effective it might be.

So I don't know exactly how many people Hugo can brainwash at once.

"At any rate, we have no way of knowing how far Hugo's influence has spread. It's best to assume this entire kingdom has been lost."

"That can't be…"

For now, our best option is to prioritize safety and regroup somewhere beyond the borders of the Analeit Kingdom.

"I can't let that happen. That's all the more reason we can't just let Hugo go! If we do something about him now, we might still be able to stop this in time!"

"No!"

Shun's logic is sound in theory, but there's a reason we can't do that!

"As long as Sophia is there, we have no chance of winning."

Sophia, once known as Negishi, is on another level of strength from us.

I fought for the humans in the war.

My goal was to make contact with Tagawa and Kushitani, who were fighting in the same battle, but all three of us found ourselves facing down a demon general called Merazophis.

Merazophis's strength was so overwhelming that it was only when we fought together that we stood even the slightest chance of landing a hit on him.

We didn't stand a chance of winning.

A single hit was all our efforts won us.

It turns out that Merazophis is a former servant of Negishi's family.

According to Potimas's research, he was originally an ordinary human but gained his current strength after Negishi's powers turned him into a vampire.

In other words, Merazophis's master Negishi is even more powerful.

I don't say this to brag, but my stats are fairly high.

And yet, I had to team up with Tagawa and Kushitani, who were likely even stronger than me, to be anywhere near even footing with Merazophis.

In that intense battle, where I thought Tagawa might be cut down at any moment, I felt the fear of death intensely even though I was providing support from the rear.

Worse yet, I feared that Tagawa and Kushitani might be killed before my very eyes, so much so that I could barely breathe.

When Kushitani was gravely injured, the fear was so strong that my insides felt frozen.

After all that, the most we could do was escape with our lives.

And yet, Negishi is even stronger than Merazophis.

We don't stand a chance of winning.

"Teacher, who in the world is she?"

Shun looks at me with alarm, perhaps finally realizing how serious I am.

"Sophia is..."

But just as I open my mouth to explain about Negishi, Leston and the others arrive.

The timing is unfortunate, but right now, escaping is more important than explaining.

Once we made it to safety, I would tell him all about it.

Or so I thought...

"Fancy meeting you here."

...until Negishi stood in our way yet again.

I've been watching everything go down by way of my clones, and damn, this is crazy!

Talk about a jam-packed event!

From Yamada's perspective, his cute little sister suddenly killed the king, then Natsume suddenly reappeared despite supposedly being exiled.

Plus, the first prince Cylis worked with Natsume to pull off a coup d'état and pinned the blame for the king's death on Yamada.

Talk about a bolt from the blue, at least for poor Yamada, y'know?

Sadly, we had no choice but to frame Yamada and force him to flee from the capital.

Poor guy...

Hmm? I can't say that when I'm the one who set him up?

Yeah, I guess you're right...

But still, if I hadn't made all this happen, things might have taken an even more tragic turn.

Natsume would've tried to get revenge on Yamada and Ms. Oka one way or another, I'm sure.

And the eldest prince, Cylis, might've acted on his inferiority complex toward his younger brothers and obsession with the throne even without our intervention.

Not to mention, Potimas was corrupting the highest echelons of the kingdom's ruling class, too!

There were already bombs all over the place.

So all we did was make those bombs go off in the most convenient directions and times for our purposes.

I got rid of the bombs for you! You're welcome!

See? I did nothing wrong!

…What do you think? Are you buying that?

No? It's still on me?

Hrm. Oh, all right. I'll admit it.

I did quite a few things wrong!

Like, we totally killed the king.

And even if he was being controlled, that poor girl who killed him might be seriously traumatized about that.

Yes, I know I've done some nasty things!

But I won't stop!

I mean, I kind of can't.

There might be a smarter way to go about this, but this is the very best I could come up with.

At any rate, we used this chaos to get rid of all the kingdom officials who were under Potimas's control, and Vampy got rid of Potimas herself.

As usual, it wasn't his real body, so he'll probably pop up in another body soon enough, but I think we at least managed to root him out of the kingdom.

With that, our mission is more or less complete.

Now all we need is for Yamada and friends to get away safely.

Without an entire kingdom behind him, Yamada shouldn't be able to do anything too crazy anymore.

We just need him to hide out someplace until everything's over.

Or so I thought, but it seems like he's having a hard time with the people Natsume brainwashed.

He can't seem to do anything against a mind-controlled Ooshima.

Hrm. I thought Yamada was strong enough to knock out Ooshima fairly easily, but maybe I overestimated him a little?

No, I guess this is more about emotions than strength.

He probably can't turn his sword on someone who's been his friend since our previous lives.

Still, though…

"Katia! Come back to your senses!"

"How very rude. My senses are fine, thank you. You are a traitor, and traitors must be punished."

What is this, a lovers' quarrel?

Ooshima shoots Fire Magic, and Yamada cancels it out with Water Magic.

It looks cool and all, but since I've gotten used to seeing all kinds of crazy next-level battles, this isn't all that exciting.

Yeah, they're definitely giving it their all, but it kinda lacks the proper tension somehow…

So it just kinda ends up looking like Yamada and Ooshima are playing around, from where I'm standing.

Again, they're really fighting their hardest, okay?

But when you've done battle with legendary-class monsters and that the like, well…y'know?

Except, as I'm kinda half-watching with a rude level of disinterest, I end up reacting too late.

WHA—?!

Ooshima blew up on purpose?!

It's a suicide attack to shake off Natsume's brainwashing!

Wait, but that definitely looks like a fatal wound to me…

Oh crap… Now I've done it…

I didn't think someone would blow themselves up just because they couldn't escape the brainwashing on their own…

"Katia?!"

Yamada runs over to the collapsing Ooshima and catches her before she hits the ground.

But since Ooshima took the full brunt of her own all-out attack, with no defenses, anyone could see that she's hurt beyond saving.

Shoot…I didn't think *this* would happen…

I guess I underestimated the strength of Ooshima's will.

I can't believe you were able to resist the brainwashing from a Seven Deadly Sins skill, even for a second…

That goes beyond unexpected.

Ahh, I'm sorry, Ms. Oka…

As I apologize silently, a soft light envelopes Yamada and Ooshima.

Healing Magic, huh? That's not going to do anything n—

Wait! This isn't Healing Magic!!

What Yamada's doing definitely isn't Healing Magic at all?!

Somehow, Ooshima's unmistakably mortal wounds are healing up.

"Ah...Shun...?"

"Katia, are you back to normal?"

"Huh? My wounds...?"

"I healed them."

"You're...so...ridicu...lous."

"Stop trying to talk. We're getting out of here."

Ooshima and Yamada start getting flirty, but I can't worry about that right now.

What just happened was so shocking that my real body jumped out of my seat.

Ooshima's wounds were definitely beyond saving.

In fact, I'm pretty sure Ooshima was already dead by the time Yamada caught her.

Normal Healing Magic can't fix fatal wounds right away, and even Miracle Magic, the advanced version of Healing Magic, can't bring people back from the dead.

There's only one skill that might be able to do that.

The Seven Heavenly Virtues skill Mercy.

That's the only skill in this world that can bring someone back from the dead.

And to think that Yamada of all people would have it...

Well, okay, I guess I had some idea that might be the case.

I actually knew that there was a human with the Mercy skill, although I didn't know who it was.

But the Seven Heavenly Virtues skills, like the Seven Deadly Sins skills, are really hard to get.

I don't think most human in this world could get it even if they deliberately tried.

Which means it's even less likely that someone would acquire it by chance.

That's why I figured there was a good chance that the person who had Mercy might be an outsider in this world: a reincarnation.

And if anyone was going to get Mercy, it probably would be Yamada.

In fact, part of the reason I had Natsume brainwash reincarnations like Ooshima and Hasebe was to figure out if any of them had Seven Heavenly Virtues skills.

Ooshima and Hasebe both turned out to be a bust, so by process of elimination, either Yamada, Ms. Oka, Tagawa, or Kushitani must be the holder of Mercy.

Personality-wise, it wouldn't be surprising if Ms. Oka had it, but since I'd never seen her use it to revive a murdered elf, that ruled her out.

That also left Tagawa and Kushitani, but Yamada seemed like a more logical fit.

But the only way to find out would be to use Appraisal on Yamada or get him to actually use it, and I couldn't very well just drop a dead body in front of him for that.

I guess this turned out to be a blessing in disguise, since I got to see him use it because of this (un)lucky break.

Although I already had a hunch it was him, I hadn't figured it into my plans since I couldn't find out for sure. Now that I know, this might be a big opportunity.

The cost of using Mercy is that one's Taboo skill levels up.

Mercy makes bringing back the dead possible, which is difficult even in the system of this world.

But once you've revived the dead, you're confronted with Taboo, which reveals the true nature of the system.

Once you find that out, you're bound to realize what it really means to bring back the dead.

D is a sick bastard, as usual.

Always out to break people's hearts.

But maybe I can use that to my advantage.

I'll lure Yamada in and have people die in front of his eyes.

No doubt he'll bring them back from the dead.

And then his Taboo level will go up.

Eventually, when it maxes out, Yamada will learn the truth of this world.

And then he'll be faced with a choice.

Will he stand against us? Or join hands with us?

I suppose pretending he didn't see anything is an option, too.

No ordinary human can carry the weight of the world on their shoulders.

And if he chooses to oppose us, then I'll crush him, of course.

But I don't think Yamada could do that.

He's a lower-middle-class kid, after all.

Sure, he's a hero or whatever now, but originally, he was just a normal boy.

So I'm sure he can't take on the fate of the world.

I'll push him into finding out the truth and get him to give up.

Yep. I was gonna have him escape and hide out somewhere, but now I'm changing the plan.

We still need him to get away from the royal capital for now, but I think I'll have Yamada see a bit more action after all.

My thoughts race as I form a new plan.

Now that Ooshima is down, the biggest obstacle to their escape is gone, so that part should be easy.

"Fancy meeting you here."

EXCUSE MEEEEE?!

Uh, Vampy? What do you think you're doing?

Why exactly are you standing in their way like some kind of big final boss?!

"Oh, here. Present for you, Ms. Oka."

"P…Potimas?!"

"I-it can't be!"

And now you're dramatically tossing her Potimas's head?!

Obviously, that's gonna freak everyone out!

Vampy! Seriously, what're you thinking?!

She licks some of Potimas's blood off her hands.

"How disgusting. Perhaps his rotten personality made his blood taste bad?"

Ew, don't lick that blood. It's dirty! Go on, spit it out!

"You did this…to Potimas?"

"What other explanation could there be?"

"But you…!"

"You're not going to say I could never kill anyone, are you? You've done plenty of killing yourself, after all. This isn't Japan. The same rules don't apply here, and you know it."

Debating with Ms. Oka is all well and good, but what are you planning to do next?

What the heck? I did explain that we were going to let Yamada and friends escape from the capital, right? She didn't forget, did she?

So why do Ms. Oka and the others look like they're about to fight Vampy?

"Ms. Oka, you want to fight me? Oh, stop. Master told me not to lay a hand on you."

See?! I knew it! I did say that, didn't I?!

Then why are you standing in their way now?!

Even those softies are gonna try to fight you if you do that!

"But I suppose you give me no choice. It's not my fault if it's just self-defense, right?"

IT TOTALLY IS, DUMBASS!

N-no, no, it'll be fine.

I'm sure even Vampy is still planning to let them go in the end.

And if it comes down to it, Phelmina will step in and stop her on my behalf! I think!

Just then, a chakram goes flying toward Yamada.

…Wait, what? Isn't that Phelmina's weapon?

Vampy alone is too powerful for these guys to take. If you add in Phelmina, there's no way for Yamada and company to win at all, is there?

Clad in black, Phelmina stops Yamada from trying to back up Ms. Oka.

An identically black-clad Wald swoops down on Hyrince, who's holding Anna.

They're not dressed in white like usual because that would stand out a bit too much for undercover work in the kingdom.

People are starting to figure out that white clothes equals the Tenth Army anyway.

I don't know if anyone in this kingdom is aware of that, but just to help avoid being found out and to fit in with Cylis's soldiers, I had them wear black.

None of that matters right now, though.

Vampy keeps canceling out Ms. Oka's magic, slowly but surely closing the distance between them.

When Vampy got the Envy skill, she also got a title that granted her the Divine Scales skill.

It's an advanced version of the Dragon Scales skill that dragons and wyrms have.

Its effects are twofold: adding scales to the user's body to increase their defense and interfering with the weaving of magic.

So it raises physical defense while also dealing with magic attacks by hindering their casting.

It's a powerful skill, one of the best defenses there is.

And as far as magic goes, by combining it with the similar effects of the Dragon Barrier skill, it can all but cancel out most magic.

Since Ms. Oka seems to have a magic-heavy build, she's a terrible match for Vampy.

Throw in the huge difference between their stats, and she pretty much has no chance of winning.

Vampy clearly realizes that and is slowly, lazily walking toward Ms. Oka.

Ms. Oka tries to stop her with Wind Magic, but since magic doesn't work on Vampy, it's literally just dust in the wind.

"Ahh!"

Finally, Vampy grabs Ms. Oka around her slim neck.

Seriously, what the heeeeell?!

What's wrong with you?!

At this rate, the adventures of Yamada and friends are gonna meet an untimely end right here!

Argh! If it's come to this, I have no choice but to show up and save them as some mysterious stranger!

But just as I'm starting to seriously consider this half-baked plan, a white wyrm comes flying in.

Isn't that…?

"Fei?"

Yamada's words overlap my thoughts as he addresses the wyrm.

Fei is Shinohara, right…?

She used to be an earth dragon, but since she made a summoning contract with Yamada the hero, she took a special route to evolve into a light wyrm.

Since it's a special evolution, she entered some kinda cocoon thing for quite a while, but it looks like the evolution finished just in the nick of time.

Seriously, talk about perfect timing!

…A little *too* perfect, don'cha think?

Maybe this is Yamada's Divine Protection skill at work again?

"Yeah, you're just in time."

While I was thinking about all that, it looks like Yamada and Shinohara were communicating telepathically.

"Shun! Mount that wyrm and get out of here!"

As the third prince Leston shouts, everyone jumps into action.

"Don't worry about us! Shun, and Hyrince, too! Take Miss Oka and run!"

"Shun! Let's go!"

Hyrince runs toward Yamada, carrying the unconscious Ms. Oka and Anna.

"Do you think we'll let you escape?"

Vampy steps in to stop them.

Uh, hello?! You're *supposed* to let them escape!

Seriously, what are you doing?!

Luckily, while Shinohara uses her dragon breath to keep Vampy and the others at bay, the others get on her back, and she flies off.

Phew. They managed to escape.

Ah, that last breath attack burned Wald pretty good…

Well, he's probably not gonna die.

Vampy and Phelmina promptly knock out Leston and the rest who stayed behind.

Phelmina quietly says something to Vampy, who brushes her off impatiently.

That's it, Phelmina! You tell her, girl!

But I'm gonna have to punish Vampy myself, too…

So I'm punishing her.

"Wait a minute! I let them go in the end, didn't I?! And besides! If we just let them leave like that, who knows what they would've done?! That's why I put a Coma status effect on Ms. Oka! Now they won't be able to make a move for a good fifteen days! See! I'm a smart girl! So you should really let me off the hook!"

A compelling testimony.

But she still needs punishment!

"Pgyaaaah!"

As Vampy shrieks like a bird being strangled, Phelmina looks on with a satisfied smirk.

You realize you were complicit in this too, though, right?

"Eeek?!"

So I punish her, too.

That being said, Yamada and the others still managed to escape in the end, and putting Ms. Oka into a deep sleep was actually a relatively smart move. I generously let them off with only a light punishment.

For the sake of Vampy and Phelmina's dignity, I won't get into the specifics.

The status condition Vampy used on Ms. Oka, Coma, is apparently an advanced version of the Sleep condition.

Just as the name implies, it puts the person into a sleep from which they can't awaken normally and it's incredibly difficult to undo.

I have no idea when she picked up a skill with a status condition like that...

In fact, I've never even heard of such a condition...

Hrm. I thought I had an idea of most skills in existence, but I guess this is a reminder that there are still skills out there I don't know about.

According to Vampy, the coma she put Ms. Oka into will wear off on its own in about fifteen days.

Why fifteen days? Because any longer than that, and her body would start rapidly deteriorating and she'd die without ever waking up.

Yikes!

I mean, I guess it makes sense. You can't eat while you're in a coma, so if it goes on for that long, it's bound to be bad news.

As long as Ms. Oka's in a coma, Yamada and the rest of them won't be able to move too much, and Ms. Oka won't be able to indoctrinate them, either.

Ms. Oka's source of information is Potimas, after all.

Knowing him, he's definitely taught her some messed-up lies.

There's no telling if that could cause Yamada and his friends to do something crazy.

In that sense, it was definitely a good call to put Ms. Oka into a coma.

It'll keep Yamada and the others pinned in place for the next fifteen days, and we can work on other stuff in the meantime.

We definitely have a lot to do.

First, there's the matter of internal affairs in the demon territory.

We've shoved all that off on Balto.

From the end of the big war till now, Mr. Oni and the rest of the commanders have been focused on postwar cleanup efforts, but that's mostly settled down now.

With Boobs back, too, we can probably return to business as usual.

Which brings us to our next step: an armed expedition to the elf village!

Yep, you heard me! The elf village is going down!

Now that the big human-demon battle is over, it's about time we get rid of that PITA Potimas, which naturally means we're embarking on a campaign to destroy the elf village.

We're not talking about the throwaway bodies Potimas keeps flinging at us.

No, this time we're gonna crush the real thing.

And that requires us to raze the whole damn elf village to the ground.

Which is exactly why we had to slow down Ms. Oka and the others, y'know?

Ms. Oka is an elf, and we can't have her getting caught up in this.

I don't know if we'll be able to keep an eye on Ms. Oka and friends while we're fighting Potimas.

It's safe to assume this is going to be a crazy-fierce battle.

I do intend to rescue the reincarnations who're being kept in the elf village, but to be totally honest, we might end up having to abandon them.

That's just how dangerous the fight with Potimas is gonna be.

So of course I want to reduce the amount of potential distractions as much as possible.

When I fight Potimas, I want to do it under ideal conditions.

Here's the thing, though. There's one guy we're gonna have to deal with for that to happen...

Dustin, the pontiff of the Word of God.

There's no way we can have an all-out war against Potimas without his help.

"...Yet another unreasonable request."

So yeah, here we are!

The Holy Kingdom of Alleius, headquarters of the smash-hit Word of God religion!

Sitting in front of me, or rather diagonally from me, is Pontiff Dustin himself.

Why isn't he right in front of me, you ask?

"You can do it, can't you? Come on, do it."

Because the one sitting directly across from him is the Demon Lord, wearing a big smile.

The pontiff is basically the head honcho of the human race.

And the Demon Lord is the head honcho of the demon race.

Normally, you'd never even expect these two to cross paths.

Yet, here they are, sitting across from each other and even having a conversation.

Normally, this kind of event would probably be one for the history books.

And in such incredible circumstances, the Demon Lord is blatantly pressuring, even threatening, the pontiff.

Man, she's something else.

In response, the pontiff heaves a heavy sigh.

"You want me to permit the demon army passage through human territory. You do understand what that would entail, do you not?"

Yep. That's the main topic for today.

Let our demon army pass through human land so we can crush the elf village, puh-leeeze.

In short, we know we're technically enemy troops, but can we come in?

Doesn't take a lot of imagination to figure out why the pontiff called it an unreasonable request.

What nation in any world would give an enemy army permission to pass its borders?

Not to mention, the Demon Lord and pontiff are officially enemies.

Since they're the representatives of the demon and human races respectively.

They're just temporarily working together because they currently have a common enemy in the elves.

The enemy of my enemy is my friend, sorta.

Although they're really all mutual enemies who aren't quite in a three-way deadlock.

Getting rid of Potimas is more urgent, so they'll cooperate a little as far as that goes, but that doesn't change the fact that they're enemies, too.

Not to mention, the demons and humans just had a big ol' war.

Asking him to grant the demon army safe passage under those circumstances is really a rash, ridiculous, reckless request.

And yet. And yet, I say!

It's really just the Demon Lord and the pontiff who are temporarily working together.

Not the demons and the humans—just the Demon Lord and the pontiff.

That part's important.

Both of them are technically at the tops of their respective races, but it's not like either of them has total control.

The Demon Lord has a pretty firm grasp thanks to her reign of terror, but that doesn't exactly mean everyone is thrilled about it.

And since the pontiff is really just in charge of a popular religion, he can't exert complete control over humans, either.

Religion is a convenient form of control for inciting people to action, but in the end, it only appeals to people's thoughts, which makes it difficult to force them to believe something they don't agree with.

Like, for instance, *Let's reconcile with the demons.*

Especially when the Word of God religion has been hyping the demons up as the sworn enemy of the human race since forever ago.

If either of them suddenly changes their official stance, they're gonna lose their ability to unify their respective bases real fast.

And since the Word of God religion is more or less built on unity, that'd basically be the end for them.

Although I'd be willing to bet some particularly faithful nobility and royals would be like, *Well, if that's what the Word of God says!* so I don't think they'd fall apart that easily.

Even though he has no lawful control over them, it's impressive that the pontiff can manipulate people this much with ideas alone.

No wonder even the Demon Lord recognizes him as a major power.

And right now, the pontiff is saying that this request is way too unreasonable.

Hrm. The Demon Lord keeps pressuring him to do it, but honestly, I don't think it's gonna work.

Even I realize this is a seriously big ask. I guess I'll just have to teleport the whole army past the human territory by myself...

"It was very difficult to lay the groundwork for this."

Wait, why is it looking more possible all of a sudden?!

...Huh? For real?

"Ahaaa! I knew you'd be able to pull it off! Yep!"

The Demon Lord beams and praises the pontiff.

But I know what she's really thinking. *Holy crap, is this guy for real...?* probably.

I mean, when I talked to him about it beforehand, this guy said even he couldn't pull off something that crazy!

But now that he's talking to the Demon Lord, here we are.

Our plan from the start was to open with a ludicrous demand, then say

Well, if you can't do that, at least help us out however you can! It's the perfect threat...ahem! I mean *negotiation tactic.*

It's a basic strategy to start by asking too much, then give your real request so it sounds doable by comparison, right?

The Demon Lord and I were laughing it up together about how he'd never be able to let the demon army pass through human territory, so we'd use that to squeeze whatever we could out of him, or at least that was the idea...

But what did this old dude just say?

It was "difficult to lay the groundwork"?

Doesn't that mean he's all ready to give us the go-ahead at any moment?

...What kind of cheater is this old man?

Listen up, reincarnations. You're better off not trying to cheat your way through politics.

You can't cheat a cheater with a half-baked plan, apparently...

"Are you sure about this, though? Wasn't this a bit of a stretch, even for the world's most popular religion?"

Ah! Demon Lord! Don't ask him that!

The pontiff's smile deepens, as if he's detected my inner panic.

"Yes, it certainly was. This favor came at a considerable expense, with no regard for the consequences. And so..." The pontiff pauses for a moment, his eyes crinkling shut with a smile. "I won't accept failure as an outcome, understand?"

EEEEEK?!

Scary?! How is this old guy so scary when he's not even strong at all?!

We came here to threaten him, but we're getting threatened instead!

"...We're not going to fail. You can count on that."

While I'm totally intimidated by the old man, the Demon Lord remains perfectly calm.

"This is the moment we've been waiting for," she continues, "for so, so long..."

Though her voice is quiet, the look in her eyes is anything but.

Wild emotions churn behind her calm expression.

"Indeed. Truly, we have waited a very, very long time for this."

The pontiff's eyes look the same.

These two have been fighting against Potimas for an incredibly long time now.

I've heard the phrase *ancient grudge* before, but their hatred for Potimas has built up for even longer than any of those.

I really hate Potimas, too, but I bet my feelings pale in comparison to theirs.

They've just had way longer to hate him.

It's even gotten to the point where they hate anything related to him.

Both the Demon Lord and the pontiff actually despise Potimas so much that they've basically committed genocide against anyone who appears to be an elf.

Although since elves are basically Potimas's spawn, I guess that's kind of inevitable.

Besides, lately, most of this elf genocide has been at the hands of the Tenth Army, under my orders... I'm not exactly in any position to judge.

But even as my mind goes off on this tangent, when I look at the Demon Lord and the pontiff gazing silently into the distance with almost nostalgic expressions, I can practically feel a cold sweat on my back.

Yeesh. We really can't afford to screw this up.

Not that I was planning on failing, of course, but y'know?

This is Potimas we're up against, remember?

There's no way that bastard doesn't have a trick or two up his sleeve.

And depending on the nature of those tricks, we might end up having to temporarily withdraw or something.

But I can't imagine saying that when I see the way the Demon Lord and the pontiff look right now...

They're giving off this "After a hundred years, we meet at last! Let's settle this once and for all!" kind of atmosphere.

...In fact, it's probably been way more than a hundred years.

I can't blame them for having some serious feelings about it.

And the success or failure of this plot to destroy Potimas rests in my hands.

Oh hey, did my stomach just start hurting all of a sudden?

'Cause that is some major pressure.

...I-it's fine, though! It's gonna be fine!

This is what I've been preparing for all this time!

I can do this!

I just gotta believe!

At least, I'm gonna keep telling myself that.

But hey, I do want to wipe Potimas out in one go if possible, just like they do.

Especially when I think about what he's put both of them through.

Potimas has caused plenty of trouble for me personally, too, so I'd like to put that to rest and leave the Demon Lord and pontiff feeling satisfied.

And since the pontiff managed to lay the groundwork for us, that should make things easier.

Our original plan assumed that even he wouldn't be able to get permission for the demon army to march through human territory.

So even though it would've been crazy tough, I was planning on teleporting the entire army directly to the elf village myself.

It would've cost tons of energy, mind you!

We just figured it was a necessary sacrifice.

But now, if we can go through the human territory, we don't have to eat that giant cost!

Which means we can put all the saved energy to other uses.

This should seriously raise our chances of defeating Potimas.

But it does cause some problems, too.

Since teleporting only takes a matter of seconds, the demon army hasn't really started to prepare to march just yet.

Except now we have to march them through human lands, which means we have to make plans for preparation and the actual march.

The Demon Lord and the pontiff are discussing the details now.

Looks like things are gonna be busy when we get back to the demon realm...

We'll have to prepare in a serious hurry.

Especially if we want to achieve the Demon Lord and pontiff's dearest wish of so many years without a hitch.

Special Chapter   THE PATH OF THE ONI

Atone.

When I close my eyes, that word rises to the surface, as if someone is speaking directly in my head.

Even when I open my eyes, the word is still there.

I can sleep and wake, and still it sticks to me without end.

Atone.

This is the effect of Taboo level 10.

The knowledge that is afforded to those who commit taboos and raise the skill level to its highest, and the cost of that knowledge.

Those who max out the Taboo skill must live with this word for the rest of their lives.

Atone.

A word directed toward all humans living in this world.

Taboo exists to make humans aware of their own sins, the actions that drove this world to the brink of destruction.

But if that's true, then what do we reincarnations who were living in a different world entirely have to atone for, and how?

The answer is…

I didn't know cleanup after a battle would be this hard.

Once I finish most of my work, I flop down exhaustedly.

Thanks to my stats and skills, my physical exhaustion isn't actually that bad.

But the mental and emotional toll is much deeper.

After all, my work right now consists of identifying those who were killed in battle, preparing condolence money to send to their relatives, and so on.

The sacrifices in the formation I led, the Eighth Army, were very extensive.

At least half of those were because I forced them to charge the enemy in what amounted to a suicide attack.

Each time I look at the list of names, I can almost hear their cries of resentment toward me.

And then there's the sight of their families clinging to their recovered bodies and sobbing.

I have to offer them my sympathies without any real emotions behind my words.

I can't let any feelings show.

I don't have the right to be emotional about it.

Because I have to be the heartless superior who cruelly sent them to their deaths.

Really, I shouldn't even be allowed to dwell on these sentiments now.

I force myself to clear my mind and focus on dealing with the aftermath.

Since I destroyed the fortress where we fought with my own hands, it's no longer strategically worth occupying.

There's no point in claiming ownership over a pile of rubble.

But we have to recover the bodies of the dead from both armies that were left on the battlefield and the supplies that were left inside the fortress.

Otherwise, battlefield looters will make off with everything.

Most of the supplies in the fortress were ruined beyond use when I blew everything up, but fortunately, there were some resources remaining that weren't destroyed in the battle, which I managed to recover.

It was collecting the corpses that was far more difficult.

Of course, it was largely the survivors and new members of the Eighth Army who were put in charge of collecting the bodies.

Most of them were friends and acquaintances of the dead.

There have been several occasions where someone discovered the body of a friend and broke down crying, unable to continue working.

I'm responsible for all this tragedy.

It's enough to put me at a loss for words.

But still, I'm not allowed to fall silent.

I have to tell the sobbing soldiers to "quit crying and work" without a shred of mercy.

If they look up at me with hatred, I glare back even more intensely.

The pressure of my glare forces them to lower their heads and surrender.

The members of the Eighth Army are a mishmash of people who never had anything to do with me.

From the very beginning, they had no reason to be loyal to me.

And now that I've forced them to march into certain death and gotten many of their comrades killed, that lack of loyalty is turning into anger and fear.

Into hatred for the meaningless deaths.

But they can't oppose me.

The resulting despair is painfully clear.

I've become an evil general who controls his soldiers with fear.

There's no justice anywhere in that picture.

But this is the path I chose.

It's way too late to turn back now.

Heaving a sigh, I stand up from the chair in my private quarters.

We're having a meeting with all the commanders today.

I leave my quarters and head for the conference room.

Along the way, I run into Mr. Merazophis.

"Hello."

"Hello."

We exchange equally brief greetings.

Mr. Merazophis is Miss Sophia's servant.

Since I became a commander, he's also been looking out for me as my senior.

He's always been a quiet man who doesn't go in for small talk, but today, he seems especially somber.

I'm sure he's feeling down for similar reasons to my own.

That normally pale face of his looks even more pallid than usual.

Together, we walk silently toward the meeting room.

When we open the door and enter, Commander Darad is already seated, with just as heavy a mood as both of us.

But unlike our mental exhaustion, Darad looks more physically drained than anything.

Unlike Merazophis and me, Commander Darad is a normal demon.

His stats are naturally lower than ours.

Between the battle and the cleanup work afterward, he must be completely worn out.

"Ah. Sir Merazophis and Sir Wrath."

Even his voice lacks its usual vigor.

This man is clearly exhausted.

"You must be working hard," I blurt out without thinking.

"Hrm. So I really do look that exhausted, eh?"

"Yes, more or less."

There'd be no point trying to deny it, so I answer honestly.

"How pathetic I am. Losing spectacularly in my biggest battle yet, then disgracing myself once again in the process of cleaning up after my mess. It's enough to make a man lose faith in himself."

Commander Darad chuckles mirthlessly.

Fortunately, Commander Kogou enters at that moment.

The giant commander senses the mood in the room and turns awkward and apologetic as he shuffles to his seat.

Commander Kogou looks pale, too.

Seems like all the commanders are being overworked to some extent.

I take my seat as well and wait for the meeting to start.

After a short while, Miss White enters the room.

Maybe it's my imagination, but it almost seemed like she glanced at Commander Kogou when she entered.

Although since her eyes are always closed, it's a bit hard to tell where she's looking.

"Heya. Looks like the gang's all here."

While I'm distracted by Miss White, Miss Ariel enters as well.

There are still some commanders missing, but I guess the rest of them aren't coming today.

More importantly, Mr. Balto looks extremely distressed next to Miss Ariel.

He's so pale, it seems like he could drop dead at any moment. Is he all right?

"The Second Army Commander isn't back yet. She won't be here today."

Miss Ariel indicates that the Second Army Commander, Sanatoria, won't be joining us.

Miss Sanatoria came to one of these meetings alone just once to report on her army's current situation, but then she went right back to the front to keep an eye on the fortress that had been overrun with monkey monsters.

Right now, she's on her way back from that fortress with the Second Army.

In the previous meeting, Miss Ariel stated that our next target is the elf village.

Some of the commanders are in contact with the elves; the former Ninth Army Commander Warkis was colluding with them.

Miss Ariel and Miss White haven't told me which ones, but I'm guessing from context that Miss Sanatoria is one of them.

It's just a guess, but I'm almost certain I'm right.

And if I can figure that much out, there's no way Miss Ariel and Miss White don't already know.

Which means that for the moment, they're knowingly letting her go free.

I can't understand why they would do that if we're on the brink of marching on the elf village to wipe out their entire race.

But knowing Miss Ariel and Miss White, I'm sure there's a very good reason that isn't immediately apparent.

"Now then, I've gathered you all here for a very important reason. We're going to discuss our plan of attack on the elf village."

Hmm? I keep my surprise to myself.

Usually, Miss Ariel leaves Mr. Balto in charge of running these meetings.

But this time, Miss Ariel herself is handling it herself.

Something strange is going on.

I can't help but get a bad feeling about it.

And more often than not, my bad feelings are right.

"There's actually been a slight change of plans. We're gonna have to move the schedule forward way sooner."

The commanders all go deathly silent, as if they've forgotten to breathe.

I can't blame them for that reaction. We've only just gotten close to being done with the postwar cleanup, and now we're going to have to march again right away.

The original plan was already pretty busy and short on time. If we're moving it up even more, then this could turn into a literal death march.

"Yeah, sorry 'bout that!"

Miss Ariel scratches her head and apologizes in a light tone.

This is no comfort at all, but she probably does genuinely feel bad on the inside.

When it comes down to it, Miss Ariel is actually a very good person.

But her apology won't make the mountain of work ahead of us any smaller.

The term *worker exploitation* flashes across my mind.

People can do amazing things if they push themselves. We managed to finish reorganizing the troops and get ready to march just in time.

It's probably because all the commanders worked together and ran around like crazy to make preparations happen.

Mr. Balto and Commander Darad were particularly cooperative; it seems to me like they became a lot more open during this period of preparation.

Even more surprisingly, Miss Sanatoria was fairly helpful, too, in spite of the fact that she's most likely working with the elves in secret.

When she got back to the Demon Lord's castle, she actually coordinated with the likes of Mr. Balto, who stayed behind to keep things running in the demon territory during the battle, and Commander Darad. She proactively participated in restoration efforts, upgrading the defenses of the troops who were getting ready to head to the elf village and so on.

Although unlike Mr. Balto and Commander Darad, she didn't offer to lend her forces to the expedition to the elf village.

Even so, she was a big help.

I guess Miss Sanatoria must have decided to cut off contact with the elves and stick with Miss Ariel.

That seems like a bit of an opportunistic move to me, but it's not really any of my business.

On the other hand, the Third Army Commander Kogou was decidedly uncooperative.

He's always been on the rebel side, and he's against this next attack, too.

That being said, although he's not actively helping, he isn't trying to stop us, either.

If someone like Mr. Balto gives him an order, he'll still do it, albeit halfheartedly.

Weak-willed. Indecisive. That's my impression of Commander Kogou.

I know it sounds a bit harsh, but I can't help it.

While the rest of us are burning the candle at both ends, he's the only commander who consistently refuses to help out.

Technically, I suppose the Ninth Army Commander Black hasn't helped, either, but he has a special position apart from the rest of us commanders.

As for the other commander with a special position, Miss White, she seems quite busy herself.

Although I've never actually seen her looking busy.

Officially, it's a mystery what kind of work Miss White's Tenth Army actually does, but I happen to know that Miss White teleports them all over the place to do various odd jobs.

The fact that I haven't seen any of the Tenth Army members during the staging period is proof in itself they've been busy.

They're here for the departure today, though.

…Although I don't see a few members, like Miss Sophia.

I'm guessing the ones who aren't here are traveling with the imperial army instead.

Before we left, Natsume—or rather Hugo—led the imperial army toward the elf village.

We'll be marching shortly after them, as the second formation in the order of battle.

I glance around the demon army as we prepare to head out.

The first thing that jumps out at me is the empire's war flags.

There are so many of them that even a cursory look leaves a strong impression.

I'd be willing to bet it was Miss White who prepared these.

We're going to pretend to be part of the imperial army while we march.

On the surface, demons and humans look exactly the same.

So as long as we display our affiliation this brazenly and spread the word in advance that the imperial army is coming, no one will be the wiser.

There are a few exceptions who visually stand out, like me, but all we have to do is cover up with full-body armor and such.

Right now, in human lands, they're probably all ready for the imperial army to come marching through.

With no idea that we're really the demon army.

I'm sure the pontiff has made sure of that.

My first impression of the pontiff was that he was an ordinary old man, or so I thought.

He didn't have any trace of the aura of the truly strong. If I wrapped my hands around his neck and squeezed just a little, I could strangle him to death easily.

Of that much I was sure.

And I wasn't wrong about that.

The pontiff is extremely weak, and I could effortlessly destroy him with a single attack.

But that's just in terms of physical strength.

Miss Ariel, of all people, calls him a monster.

I got a brief but vivid glimpse of that side of him.

"That is precisely why I will not allow the mountains of sacrifices to have died in vain."

I'm sure the pontiff had no idea how much those words shook me to my core.

I first met the pontiff when Miss White and Miss Ariel took me along to visit the Holy Kingdom of Alleius.

Right before the war, it was a meeting between sworn enemies: the head of the demons and the leader of the Word of God religion, who could essentially be called the leader of the humans.

For some reason, I was also allowed to sit in on this fateful meeting.

Miss Ariel and the pontiff previously came to the consensus that they would work together after the war to take down the elves as a united front, and they evidently forged a secret pact.

So the goal of this meeting was to pool their ideas and frankly discuss a plan of action for after the war and after defeating the elves.

Miss Ariel is a true living witness, a being who's been around since before the system was created.

And from what she's told me, the pontiff has a highly unusual skill that allows him to be reborn over and over with memories of all his previous lives intact.

That means he's a living witness to history like Ariel, even if he's been reborn many times instead of surviving all the while.

And if he knows the real history of this world, that means he knows all about the system, too.

Taboo taught me the truth of the system.

Namely, that the foolish actions of humans brought this world to the brink of destruction, and a lone goddess sacrificed herself in order to keep that destruction at bay.

But that's only a temporary solution, and this world is still in danger of falling apart.

The system is essentially an enormous spell that takes the experience points that every living being builds up throughout their life, the power reflected in their stats and skills, and recovers it after that being's death, using it to restore the world and keep it from falling into ruin.

Miss Ariel and the pontiff know the truth about this system.

That's why Miss Ariel is pitting demons against humans as the Demon Lord and providing the system with more energy by causing mass deaths.

And the reason the Word of God religion teaches followers to train their skills and hear "God's voice" more often is to increase the amount of energy they provide the system over the course of their lives.

As the residents of this world grow up, they hear announcements each time they gain new skills, level up, and so on within the system.

Very few people find it strange to consider that the voice of God.

They've been hearing it all their lives, after all.

But when the other reincarnations learn about the rules of the Word of God, they might just think that this world has some very strange beliefs.

If I found out about that creed without knowing anything else, I'm sure I would've thought the same thing.

With other reincarnations, we might have even made jokes about it.

The Word of God religion is so silly, we'd say.

But knowing the truth, it's nothing to laugh about.

The Word of God actually uses the framework of religion to extort all of humanity.

It tells them to become part of the foundation for the world.

Since they were raised with this creed from birth, indoctrinated by it, they fully believe they're following the doctrines of the Word of God of their own free will.

It's extremely effective. Terrifyingly so, in fact.

I'm sure it unsettles me because it treats lives as consumable goods.

It almost feels like a farm: raising livestock in the form of humans and shipping them out to be eaten.

And it's all the more unsettling since the humans don't know they're being raised as livestock at all…

But the person who created this farm is none other than the pontiff of the Word of God.

The more I learn about that religion, the more I realize how terrifying the pontiff is.

It's his organizational capability that makes him so scary.

The Word of God religion has influence over almost every human nation.

One of the only exceptions is Sariella, a nation that worships the Goddess instead, but there are churches in every other human state.

Even the smallest villages have chapels, spreading the roots of the Word of God religion.

Young children receive the blessing of the Church and grow up hearing its teachings.

By the time they reach adulthood, they're faithful believers in the Word of God.

That's how the Church grasps people's hearts and gains a soft grip of control over humanity.

Not only that, but the churches scattered throughout the world are either used as information-gathering centers or stopping points through which information is relayed.

Apparently, most people who work under the Church acquire the skill Fartalk, an advanced version of Telepathy. This skill allows its users to communicate with one another over a long distance.

They use this skill to relay information, telephone game–style, all the way to the Word of God headquarters in the Holy Kingdom of Alleius.

It may not quite be real-time updates, but it's still a very fast way of gathering information from distant lands.

The pontiff knows very well just how incredibly valuable new information can be.

In this world without cars or airplanes, travel takes a long time.

Aside from exceptions like teleport gates and Fartalk, the fastest way to convey information is by courier on horseback, but even that is often too slow.

But by putting Fartalk users in every nation, the pontiff can cut down the delay in transmitting information to the absolute minimum.

Then he analyzes that information and makes his moves accordingly.

On top of that, he also has other mechanisms in place that solidify the Church.

Most importantly of all, while these structures require a lot of people, what they *don't* require is any particular talent.

Fartalk is an advanced skill, but as long as one learns Telepathy, all that's required is practice.

Similarly, all the skills required to work for this religious organization are perfectly ordinary.

Anyone could learn them if they put their mind to it.

In other words, it's a job anyone can do.

And that's really important.

Because it means he can train any number of replacements.

Instead of putting management of the organization in the hands of one amazing person, he uses the masses to support it.

And since anyone can do it, vacancies are easily covered, with plenty of replacements ready to fill the void.

If one person is lost, someone else can step into their shoes.

Even the pontiff himself is no exception to that rule; when the man who inherited the name Dustin is absent, a different pontiff takes over the role.

And even at those times when Dustin wasn't at the head, the Word of God church never wavered.

The foundation of this religion is that frighteningly solid and unshakable.

The Word of God religion has been a fixture for hundreds of years, cementing its place as a permanent part of human society.

Yes, the pontiff is undoubtedly a remarkable man.

But instead of his own power, he uses other people to control humanity.

He truly is a king among men.

His nature makes him stand out even among all the incredible people I've met.

Miss Ariel, Miss White, Miss Sophia, Mr. Merazophis…all of them are incredibly powerful in their own right, so they never depend on those below them.

Since they're perfect on their own, as complete individuals, they never bothered to become kings who command others with their strength.

The person I've met who was most suited to the role of king was probably the late Mr. Agner, the First Army Commander.

Mr. Agner didn't just lead the First Army—he led the demon race as a whole with great care.

But even then, I have to admit that Mr. Agner's organization was still utterly dependent on his strength and the authority that came with it.

Without him, his followers couldn't stand on their own.

But the pontiff's control isn't so fragile that things would fall apart after the loss of a single person.

He probably figured out his own strengths and limits from the start and focused on building up an organization right away.

He has incredible insight that allows him to predict future developments.

And since he really did manage to make the Word of God religion so massive, there's no doubt that he has unbelievable shrewdness and strategy.

Now, most of this is just what I learned from Miss Ariel.

Once I had her teach me about the Word of God religion, I thought I understood how amazing the pontiff was.

…But when I met him in person, I realized I still had a lot to learn.

"We're going to kill the hero. That's already set in stone."

"But if you do that, humanity will no longer be able to stand against you, the Demon Lord. Is this not perhaps a tad bit too one-sided?"

"And how much energy do you think the hero would waste in order to confront me? We'd both be better off without that happening, don't you think?"

"…I see. So you will not only kill the hero, but eliminate the very framework of heroes entirely?"

"That's the plan."

"What are the merits and demerits of doing so?"

The pontiff and Miss Ariel were candidly discussing how to handle the hero. From what I'd heard, that hero was the older brother of my best friend from my previous life, Shun.

And the pontiff was using the elimination of a human-trafficking organization secretly run by the elves as a way to have that hero build up battle experience and popularity alike.

Since the conflict with the demons was limited to a cold war for the time being, there was nowhere for the hero to make a name for himself.

So the pontiff decided to kill three birds with one stone: get the hero more experience in battle, spread the word of his accomplishments, and crush the plot of the elves all at once.

As a result, Julius the hero became very popular, and by gaining experience by fighting the human-trafficking organization, he raised his level to be on par with previous heroes.

And then, having overseen the hero's growth in this way, the pontiff cast him aside without a second thought when confronted with the benefits of doing so.

"You wish me to declare Hugo Baint Renxandt the new hero?"

"That's right. The real one is Schlain Zagan Analeit."

"And why would we hide that?"

"Because Hugo is a pawn to our dear White. Although I don't think he knows it. Calling a human we can completely control the official hero will make things much easier for us."

"I see. Does this have anything to do with the suspicious activity Potimas has been getting up to in the Analeit Kingdom?"

"It sure does. If we wanna kick Potimas out of the Analeit Kingdom, we're gonna have to cause some serious trouble there first. And we'll need the whole of society to believe that Hugo is in the right."

"So you've concluded that the fastest and most effective way to build that trust is by declaring Prince Hugo the hero, hmm?"

"I'm glad you're so quick on the uptake."

"But if that lie is exposed, the Word of God religion will lose a great deal of credibility. How do you intend to compensate for that?"

"Stamping out the elves is a pretty good payoff, don't you think? We're planning on using Hugo for that, too, so your church can take half the credit since you helped out. If anything goes wrong, just claim that Hugo brainwashed you."

He wouldn't hesitate to falsify the real hero if it benefited his purposes.

Or plunge an entire kingdom into chaos if it meant defeating Potimas.

On the one hand, you could say he has a good grasp of the big picture.

On the other hand, it's horribly machinelike, viewing people's lives as nothing more than numbers.

If discarding one person would save two or more people, then he'd discard that person without hesitation, even if it's the hero.

Of course, if the hero's usefulness outweighed the people who would be saved, I imagine he would just as soon not cast him aside.

But that wouldn't be because he's considering the individual—no, all that matters would be the abilities of the chess piece called the hero.

A political monster, putting aside any personal feelings or human kindness.

To the human race, he is a king, an absolute guardian, an ally.

And yet, he himself lacks humanity in his principles.

What kind of sick joke is it that the man who leads the human race has no humanity himself?

I couldn't wrap my head around it.

So I ended up blurting out a comment.

"You say you want to protect humanity, but you're willing to offer them up so easily."

He responded:

"If the only way to save the many is to kill the few, then I will kill the few without hesitation."

Then Miss Sophia snorted.

"What a piece of work, slaughtering the people he's supposed to save."

From what I've been told, Miss Sophia's hometown was destroyed by a sect of the Word of God religion, and Potimas took advantage of the confusion to murder her parents.

It's understandable that she'd hold resentment against the Church.

But the pontiff responded calmly to Sophia's accusation, too.

"That is precisely why I will not allow the mountains of sacrifices to have died in vain."

That idea stunned me into silence.

Not only was he not proud of what he'd done, but it seemed almost as if he was apologizing to the mountains of dead he'd created.

But he still refused to stop.

If he did, he would be letting all those deaths, those sacrifices, go to waste.

Maybe this was the pontiff's form of atonement.

An endless atonement, the course of which leads him to accumulating even more sins that need to be answered for.

Yet, he continues, knowing there will be no end, no forgiveness.

How harsh must that experience be?

It made me shudder.

That might have been the first time I realized just how unknowable the pontiff really is.

I hadn't decided how to live my life.

I was born as a goblin, then the goblin village where I was raised was destroyed, and I was forced to work for Buirimus, the very man who massacred my village.

Then I gained the Wrath skill, escaped from Buirimus's enslavement, and managed to avenge my fallen brethren.

But after that, I half lost my mind because of Wrath and went around killing everything in sight.

The fact that I met Miss White and the others and had Wrath sealed away to regain my senses was nothing short of a miracle.

If I had continued wandering around half-mad, I probably would have soon run out of strength and died in a ditch.

I am lucky to be alive.

Unlike the people I killed.

Since I had the good fortune to be saved, I thought it was my duty to keep on living.

And if I was going to keep living, I wanted to accomplish something.

But I hadn't figured out what exactly I should do.

I just followed Miss Ariel, Miss White, and the others.

They were trying to do something incredible and save the world, and I'd just been going along for the ride in some small way.

Without ever facing the sins I committed.

All I did was look on in admiration at people who knew what they wanted and pursued it without hesitation.

But part of me questioned it.

Did someone as aimless as me really have any right to fight at their side?

I couldn't help worrying about it.

Could taking people's lives for the greater good really be called justice?

I'm sure Miss Ariel and Miss White already had that all figured out.

But I couldn't reach a conclusion so easily.

In my old life, I hated anything I thought was wrong.

I was borderline obsessed with ensuring that everything I did was right.

But when I was controlled by Wrath and murdered innocent people, that was obviously wrong.

Ever since then, I'd lost sight of how I wanted to live.

I'd already strayed from the path of righteousness.

I couldn't find a new path to follow and just trailed after the backs of Miss Ariel and Miss White, which I could see in the distance.

In that moment, the pontiff's words were like a beacon of light.

Knowing that what you're doing isn't right, knowing that it's a sin, you keep pushing forward for the greater good.

The pontiff showed me that this, too, is one way to live.

I'm sure it will be a painful, challenging path.

But in that moment, I realized that was the path I should choose to move forward.

Atone.

That word that echoes from Taboo.

All right, then.

I'll atone.

I'll steel myself to commit even more sins and atone for those, too.

To make up for the deaths of the innocent people I killed.

To make sure they didn't die in vain.

No, even that is self-serving.

Calling it atonement is far too grandiose.

I will take countless lives for my own selfish reasons.

I won't apologize.

And I won't look back anymore.

I'll continue adding to those mountains of bodies.

And I'll serve the greater good.

That's the only way I can move forward.

Thus, I led the Eighth Army in the war and ensured countless sacrifices on both sides.

And now, I'm leading the march to the elf village.

Our goal is to exterminate the elves.

To commit genocide against an entire race.

I'm sure many lives will be lost.

"Move out!"

On Miss Ariel's cue, I begin walking.

Forward, always forward.

I won't stop ever again.

5   Doing Traffic Control and Executions for a Living

Sooo buuusyyyy.

I am sooo, sooo buuusyyyy.

Buuusy spiiideeeer.

Lyrics by yours truly.

Um, hello? Where are my days off?

My weekends?

Holidays?

What about summer break, winter break, spring break, or Golden Week?!

I've been working nonstop for days on end here!

Does the Labor Standards Act not apply to the demon army?!

This is all that stupid pontiff's fault for being too good at what he does.

In theory, having an exceptionally talented business partner seems great, but not when that means you have to work way faster just to keep up…

Come on. Can nothing be easy?

This just goes to show that dealing with other people never leads to anything good.

That is to say, being a loner shut-in is the ideal lifestyle!

When you get involved with other people's business, they'll stick you with a bunch of work, and then you end up busy like me.

So obviously, it's better to do whatever you want, on your own, at your own pace!

That way, if anything fails, you only have yourself to blame.

And while you can blame yourself, other people aren't going to blame you. Self-responsibility.

What a wonderful phrase…

So what am I trying to say, exactly?

Basically, I just don't wanna screw this up and have the pontiff get mad at me…

Like, all this time, I've mostly just been running around doing whatever I want on my own terms, yeah?

So even if I failed, that was no one's business but my own.

But what will the pontiff think if I fail this time around?

From his perspective, the Demon Lord is the leader of our faction, of course.

So the blame for failure would land squarely on the Demon Lord.

Urgh, my stomach hurts.

Which is exactly why I've been busting my hump like crazy around here.

Unlike the teleportation I was planning on, marching through the human territory is going to take a few days. With my teleport magic, it would've been instant.

And since it'll take a few extra days, that means we have to speed things along accordingly.

Plus, we have to secure rations for the trip and stuff.

Well, I've got Balto working on that part.

And each individual army is preparing on their own otherwise.

Then what exactly have I been doing, you ask? Well, tons of stuff that no one else but me could do, duuuh.

First, taking care of a few things in the empire.

Since we were planning to travel by teleportation, I didn't think about going through the empire, which means I haven't done any setup ahead of time whatsoever.

We told the pontiff that we poached Natsume for our army, so he seems to think that the empire is under our jurisdiction or something.

Which is to say, he told us at the meeting that he'd leave it up to us.

Thanks, but I really wish you wouldn't…

Natsume's Lust skill can only provide complete control over a few brainwashed people at a time.

There's no real limit on the number in theory, but unfortunately, it takes a long time to set everything up for a full brainwash.

It's definitely not the kind of thing where he snaps his fingers and goes *Voila! You are now under my hypnosis!*

He has to use it on them repeatedly over time for the effect to really sink in.

If he just uses it once, the effect will expire, and they'll be back to normal in no time.

And even when they've been completely brainwashed, the effect will get weaker over time if it's not refreshed.

Although when the brainwashing effect has been applied that many times, it should take an equally long time for the person to come back to their senses. And if someone tries to force them to snap out of it with Healing Magic or something, it'll be more difficult the longer they've been in the brainwashed state.

Unlike me, our pal Natsume only has one body, and even teleporting him around with me to brainwash various people has its limits.

For one thing, Natsume only has so much MP.

Yep, the Lust skill requires MP to use.

And since Natsume's MP is so limited, we have to carefully pick and choose who we brainwash.

We've done it to the most important people in the empire already, mostly to solidify Natsume's position.

You know, like Natsume's father, the sword-king of the empire.

Also, super-influential lords and stuff like that.

Mostly just civil officials, though.

Man, I gotta tell ya, the internal affairs of the empire have gotten super corrupted…

Most of 'em were in a nasty all-out political war.

The civil officials were all skimming off the top, dealing out injustices, all that kind of stuff.

Meanwhile, the military generals are so muscle-headed that the officials managed to deceive them into leaving for far-off areas and so on, keeping their power in check.

The sword-king tried to wrangle the military officers under control and restrain the corrupt officials, but the strength-obsessed generals don't accept the sword-king because they consider him to be too political.

So instead of skillfully handling anyone, the king here is totally isolated.

And now the generals are distancing themselves from the sword-king and refusing to help keep the peace in the capital.

Which means the corrupt civil officials can do whatever they want.

Yeah, the whole thing is pretty hilarious.

I could definitely picture an epic period drama or movie about it with the sword-king as the protagonist.

Anyway, since that's what was up in the empire, all we had to do was convince those corrupt officials to come over to our side, and everything worked out fine.

We didn't even have to brainwash all of them—some were willing to do what we asked if we just handed them a bribe.

I mean, that made things easy for me and all, but yikes…

Mr. Sword-King, you can cry if you want to.

You're being brainwashed by your own son, for one thing.

Huh? Who made him do that, you ask?

Oh yeah, that was me.

The mysterious woman pulling the strings of a corrupted empire.

You can call me the femme fatale of ruining royal courts if you want, okay?

So yeah, the empire is firmly under our control now, but it's not exactly airtight.

For instance, we've got over half the civil officials on our side, but we left the generals alone.

Most of them have territory that's either close to or directly on the border with the demon realm.

If we want to get through the empire, we're going to have to pass through their land one way or another.

So I'm gonna have to do something about that.

Also, we're going to use a teleport gate to go from the empire to the next human nation.

We're obviously not gonna march from the demon realm all the way to the elf village across a whole continent.

The empire is big enough that it has multiple teleport gates, but after the big war and all, the waiting list to use them is crazy long.

There are reinforcements sent to the empire from other nations who are now trying to get home, adventurers who enlisted as volunteer soldiers, and so forth and so on.

On top of that, there's distribution of goods that was halted during the war in favor of the transportation of soldiers.

Basically, since teleport gates are so convenient, they naturally see lots of traffic during emergencies like this one.

Plus, now they also need to be used to teleport Natsume and the imperial army toward the elf village, meaning there's serious congestion.

And we have to squeeze our way in to use one somehow.

Even though they're all super booked already.

We need to cut in line in front of all those people waiting to use the teleport gate.

Us, an entire army.

Ha-ha-ha. Yeah, this is gonna require some fancy footwork!

So I've had the Tenth Army running around to solve all kinds of problems within the empire.

How did I solve them, exactly? Well, there are some things in this world you're better off not knowing. That's all I'm gonna say.

Like why a certain general and his extended family all went mysteriously missing, for instance.

Look, the literal fate of the world is at stake here—we've gotta do whatever it takes.

And there's no time to waste…

Meaning I can't be wasting all of it on the empire anyway.

We're still not done in the Analeit Kingdom, for one thing.

Based on my original plans, I should be focusing on there by now.

But because of a sudden change in plans that came up with that part, I've had to divert some resources over there, too.

Basically, I'm now stuck fighting a war on two fronts over here.

No wonder I'm so freakin' busy!

Anyway, here we are in the Analeit Kingdom.

Specifically, the royal castle where an uprising took place the other day.

It's late at night, and everyone is sound asleep.

Although that being said, this place is a little *too* quiet.

After all, it's a stupidly massive castle, and there's only a handful of people in it at present.

So the silence is so overwhelming, it's almost deafening.

Later tonight, Yamada and friends should be breaking into this castle.

I know this because we just announced that the third prince Leston and Ooshima's duke and duchess parents, who we captured during the uprising, are going to be executed.

Knowing Yamada and Ooshima's personalities, they're definitely going to try to launch a rescue.

In fact, my clones that are watching Yamada and friends already saw them leaving their hideout.

So I more or less emptied out the castle to make it easier to greet them.

Why would I go through all that trouble, you ask? Well, I guess you could call it an experiment.

To be totally honest, technically, I don't really *have* to do this particular experiment… But it'll make for useful insurance when I fight Potimas, or rather totally destroy him.

If this experiment succeeds, it'll open up a new option for me.

Although even if it does succeed, I don't really wanna take that option if I can help it.

Let's just say it's definitely a last resort.

Uh, well, hrmmm…the experiment is definitely reason numero uno, but there are a bunch of other small reasons, too, and they all add up to it making more sense to do than not.

Like, it'll keep Yamada and friends even more occupied, for instance.

But did I really have to force it into my schedule during this ridiculously busy period? Uh…I almost kinda feel like I didn't?

…Honestly, I was kinda obsessed with carrying out every single project I had planned, but I probably could've put off or postponed a few of the less important ones, huh?

…Okay, maybe. But still!

It was already planned, so I figured I should still do it!

If I put it off or postponed it, my plans would get more messed up down the line!

So in other words, what I'm saying here is that it's really better if I do it! Yeah!

No doubt about it.

As I nod silently to myself in affirmation, I sense a disturbance in the f— um, in space.

Hrm? Someone's trying to teleport in here?

If anyone's gonna show up via teleportation right now, I'd guess it would be Güli-güli?

No, wait, I take it back.

The construction of this teleportation portal is on a lesser skill level from Güli-güli's.

Frankly, it's kinda messy.

Besides, if it was Güli-güli, he'd already be here moments after I sensed him coming.

If it's taking this long for them to show up, it can't be him.

I guess the construction is half-decent, objectively speaking, but considering that Güli-güli is a literal god, obviously, it's gonna pale in comparison.

Actually, just the fact that they can use Spatial Magic at all means they're pretty damn skilled.

Me and Güli-güli are exceptions, but usually, Spatial Magic isn't the kinda thing you can just use willy-nilly. Only a few people in this world can use it at all.

Even the Demon Lord can only just barely use basic Spatial Magic, y'know?

Anyway, enough defending this unknown user for whatever reason. Who the heck is gonna show up? I brace myself.

And soon, an old man appears.

Ahh, I knew it. This guy.

I've seen this old geezer before.

Quite a few times, in fact.

Apparently, he's called Ronandt or something.

Well, his name doesn't really matter, but he is the leading imperial court mage and definitely the strongest guy in the empire.

In fact, as far as magic goes, he's probably the strongest human of all.

He was also Julius the hero's magic teacher and has lots of connections besides.

I definitely have him pegged as one of humanity's major players.

After all, he's also basically the authority on Spatial Magic, with the highest skill level of any human I've ever seen.

So when someone was teleporting here, he was my number one guess.

The question is, why would this geezer show up here at this particular moment?

I thought he was traveling with Natsume and the imperial army.

Since he's way stronger than Natsume, we couldn't brainwash him or anything, but it'd be a shame to let his power go to waste, so we just ordered him to join the expedition.

Easy enough to do, since we've got the sword-king of the empire in our hands.

And at the moment, the imperial army is supposed to be marching toward the elf village.

Then what exactly is this old man doing here and not with them?

Hrm. Well, I guess the obvious assumption is that he's here to help Yamada and company, right?

I don't think he's actually met Yamada before, but he did teach his older brother.

And he has met Hyrince, who's traveling with Yamada right now.

…Okay, but would he really teleport here in such a hurry just for that?

It doesn't quite add up.

Oh well. Throwing one old man into the mix won't change what I have to do—I guess it's no big deal.

The only person I really need for this experiment is Yamada anyway.

Frankly, it doesn't really matter how much power he has on his side.

'Cause this castle is practically empty, remember?

There's not gonna be a big battle.

So it doesn't make a difference if the old man joins them.

Sorry you went to all the trouble, gramps, but there's nothing for you to do here, okay?

The old man is standing on top of the royal castle.

Taking the utmost care not to be noticed, I hide my presence and watch him.

He doesn't move, either, probably sensing what's inside the castle.

Before long, his brow furrows suspiciously.

Well, yeah. The castle is basically empty right now.

If he showed up to save the day only to find the place devoid of enemies, it's no wonder he'd react to that.

"Eh, it's fine."

IS IT, THOUGH?!

I silently scream at the old man's careless mumbling.

Come on, use your head a little more!

There's obviously something wrong with the castle being abandoned, right?!

Should you really just leave it at that?!

Come on, let's see you act like the big shot imperial mage or whatever! Do SOMETHING!

But instead, the old man loses interest in the inside of the castle and starts gazing up at the sky instead.

Oof, this guy's an oddball all right!

You know the type.

People who march to the beat of their own drum and no one else's.

Usually, people like that are incapable of working in groups and cooperating with others.

Ugh. Really now, you should try to make peace with others a little more, like me.

So? Is this guy waiting for Yamada and the others to show up?

Maybe he's planning to meet up with them and break into the castle together.

Although I doubt whether this guy will actually be able to work together with Yamada and his crew.

They're definitely gonna have a falling out, if you ask me.

See? Look, Yamada showed up and the old guy's firing magic at... I'm sorry, what?

Hmm? Hmmmm?

What the hell is this geezer doing?

He's shooting magic...at Yamada and his friends...? What?

Whaaat?

Unreal.

Why would you even do that?

Like, the old man is flying through the air and just firing off a barrage of magic at them.

Yamada and his group are riding on Shinohara in dragon form, high in the sky.

And now they're getting laser beams shot at them.

Shinohara is pretty high up there, but the laser's aim is really accurate.

She's dodging around like crazy.

Well, I guess that's some impressive marksmanship, fitting for a big shot imperial mage.

But I probably shouldn't be admiring that right now, huh?

I don't know why the old man's attacking Team Yamada, but at this rate, they might just straight up run away.

He's definitely keeping them at bay right now.

Shinoda's trying to close the distance, but getting closer means pushing deeper into the old man's magic range, making them a target for bigger and stronger spells. Plus, the time from casting to impact is only going to get shorter.

In other words, it'll make it harder to dodge, and deal more damage if it hits.

Some manga protagonist once said that a knife is faster than a gun in close combat, or something, but that definitely doesn't equate to guns being totally useless in close quarters.

The phrase *point-blank shot* exists for a reason.

When you're fighting a really skilled mage, you've gotta get close to them to have a chance at winning, but just getting close isn't some automatic guarantee of victory.

Will Yamada be able to get close to the old man?

Actually, I kinda need him to get close and win, or it'll screw up my plans!

Beams of light shoot out of the old man's cane, and Shinohara dodges them as she presses closer.

But just like I feared, her ability to avoid them reaches a limit as she gets closer, and one of the lasers grazes Yamada's cheek.

He put up a barrier to protect himself, but it looks like it didn't fully prevent him from getting hit: Blood starts to trickle down his cheek.

Somehow, that actually seems to boost Shinohara's determination, and she starts charging ahead.

She gives up on dodging completely and zooms straight toward the old man.

But that'll just make her the perfect target.

Sure enough, he shoots a laser beam toward Shinohara.

Yamada produces a shield of light to block the laser.

Ah, so they're planning on blocking like this to close the distance.

A few more laser beams shoot out, and Yamada blocks each of them.

Then, once they've gotten close enough, Yamada jumps off Shinohara's back and swings his sword down at the old man!

Wow. That's some action movie–level stuff.

But unfortunately, the old man still outclasses him.

Yamada's sword only cuts through air.

From his point of view, Yamada probably has no clue what happened, but I had a perfectly clear shot of the moment.

It was Short-Range Teleport.

The old man used teleportation to get behind Yamada.

"Hmm. Well, I suppose that earns passing marks."

Now he's saying something obnoxious to Yamada.

In the next moment, he fires another barrage of magic at our young hero.

Looks like he's using low-level magic at rapid-fire speed.

The spells you learn as your magic skills level up are generally more powerful, but they also take more time to invoke.

So instead, the old man is using weaker low-level spells in large quantities and at high speed to turn this into a bullet hell game for Yamada.

For a human, this old guy is pretty damn good.

Yamada uses his sword and those magic light shields from before to block them.

But he can just barely keep up with the defense.

I don't see him being able to counterattack, and in fact, even his defenses won't last much longer.

"Yaaaah!"

The situation changes in the form of Hyrince jumping down from Shinohara's back.

He brings down his blade toward the old man's head as he descends.

Just like he did with Yamada moments ago, the old man escapes using Short-Range Teleport.

The geezer teleports behind Yamada.

Hyrince lands, and he and Yamada shift their stances.

They're trying to reset, I guess.

But now, Shinohara is in the sky above the old man, and Ooshima is on her back, both ready to attack.

One against four.

Even this guy will have trouble dealing with those odds.

And it looks like he realizes it, too.

"Oh dear… This is too much. You got me, you got me. This old man is retreating."

With that, he teleports away.

A real Teleport this time, not just Short-Range.

Since he was already starting to form the spell for it right after he dodged Hyrince's attack with Short-Range Teleport…

…He must've known at that moment that he couldn't win.

……So, uh.

What exactly did he come to do in the first place?

The weird old geezer attack aside, Yamada and friends have arrived to rescue their family members from being executed.

I'm sure that old man's attack caught them off guard. Hell, I wasn't even expecting it.

Seriously, what was that guy thinking…?

Team Yamada warily searches inside the empty castle.

They're proceeding with caution, clearly expecting a trap.

But this isn't really a trap. Not exactly.

So they reach the throne room without any issues.

There, the first prince Cylis is sitting on the throne, waiting for them.

Lined up in front of him are the people who were announced to be executed: the third prince Leston, the duke and his wife, and some older lady named Klevea.

This Klevea person was originally Yamada's maid.

She's a bit too well-built to be a maid, if you ask me, but apparently, she used to be a soldier.

She was captured along with Leston during the uprising, so I threw her in with the rest of the bunch.

The executioners stand behind the four captives.

And as soon as Yamada's crew enters the room, they swing their swords before anyone can stop them and behead the four victims right before their eyes.

Then Yamada goes running up in a hurry and uses a certain skill.

The resurrection skill: Mercy.

As I watch in secret, the third prince and the other captives are all brought back to life.

Man, that's way too easy.

We're talking about people's lives here.

But divine power can manipulate even life and death.

It's kind of unsettling, seeing D's ridiculous power on display like this.

I mean, it's not like I *couldn't* bring back the dead.

But that's only in this world, where the system exists.

My power is limited, and it only works because the concepts of life and death are different in this world than others.

There's no way I'd be able to bring back the dead in a world without this system, no matter how hard I tried.

And D built that whole system from scratch.

Even before I became a god, I could never figure out just how strong D was, but even as a god myself, I have yet to find any limits to D's power.

It's seriously terrifying.

Bringing back the dead is literally the work of miracles, but Yamada can do it for only a small cost.

He has no idea just how messed up that is.

A feat like that should cost way more than just raising Taboo's level a bunch.

Besides, I wouldn't be so obsessed with staying alive in the first place if it was that easy to bring people back.

Hrm.

I kept it to four people just in case Yamada ran out of MP, but maybe I should've thrown in a few more?

From what I can tell, it doesn't look like his Taboo skill maxed out.

It probably still went up four levels, though, so this whole exercise wasn't a waste.

Besides, leveling Yamada's Taboo skill is just a bonus.

This whole thing is just a sideshow, really.

If it failed, it wouldn't have been that big of a deal.

My experiment is complete anyway.

I take a peek at the revived third prince's soul.

Yep.

Potimas's soul has been ripped out of him.

All I really needed to know was if you could get rid of Potimas's influence by dying once.

That was the main goal of this experiment: What happens if you kill someone who's got a Potimas parasite, then bring them back to life?

And now we know.

Based on how the system works, I had a hunch that skills wouldn't continue to affect the soul of someone who's died, but now I know for sure.

So what does this mean, exactly? If you kill someone and bring them back to life, they can be freed from Potimas's control.

It's a pretty violent method, but now I know that if it comes down to it, there's at least one way to free Ms. Oka from Potimas's clutches.

…Although since that method would mean killing Ms. Oka, albeit temporarily, I would prefer not to do it, if possible.

Plus, it was humans we used in this experiment, not elves.

Since humans are outside the scope of Potimas's Kin Control, I imagine it might be harder for him to parasitically control them.

Which means that even if killing them once works for humans, it might not be the same for elves.

So I should probably keep this as an absolute last resort after all.

Well, I'm all good here. Now I just need to make sure Yamada and friends escape safely.

"Shun, go check on the teleport gate, please. I assume it's broken and won't work, but just to be sure. I'll stay here and keep an eye on Leston and the others."

"All right."

Sounds like Yamada and his little friends are gonna go check on the teleport gate.

It's one of the major forms of transportation in this world.

Since you can cross from one continent to another in an instant, it's definitely very convenient.

If you want to get to the other continent without a teleport gate, you have to either cross an ocean teeming with water dragons or make your way through the Great Elroe Labyrinth.

And the ocean's basically impossible, leaving the labyrinth as the only real option.

So Yamada goes to check on the teleport gate.

Of course, I already had Natsume destroy it.

I'm not gonna let them cross continents that easily.

But I'm guessing the only reason that guy suggested the check is just to be sure, like he said, and to be able to move a little more freely.

The door to the room I'm in opens.

Without even a knock. Talk about rude.

"That was in poor taste, even for you."

And that's the first thing he says when he comes through the door.

You mad?

Oh yeah, he mad.

As further proof, he stomps into the room and sits down in the chair across from me, crassly and violently.

"You pitted Sir Ronandt, Julius's master, against Julius's younger brother Shun. I'm sure it made for quite a dramatic show, but consider the feelings of those of us who had to participate. Do you have any idea how Sir Ronandt must have felt when he chose to retreat?"

Well, no, not really.

That guy showed up here of his own accord.

Not my problem. Not my business. Not my fault.

But in order to make it clear that I won't succumb to pressure, I ignore him and sip my tea.

"That is downright inhuman."

Uh, yeah. Sorry.

I'm not a human, and I never was.

But it still doesn't feel great to be insulted like that.

Even I'm bound to get annoyed with all these false accusations flying.

"And you're not very godly, Black."

So I give him a piece of my mind, too.

Because the man called Hyrince who's sitting in front of me is really a clone of Black, also known as Güli-güli.

"That's true. I have had the same thought. You are but newly made, yet you are far more godlike than I." Güli-güli heaves a deep sigh. "And I do know that no matter what I say now, I am just taking it out on you. I understand that the path you have chosen is the best way forward. And yet, even so…I find it difficult to restrain these emotions."

He's grieving.

Well, I can't blame him. He was playing the part of the previous hero Julius's old friend but had to let him die in front of his eyes, and now Julius's younger brother is going through all kinds of tough times. I'm sure it must practically unbearable to watch up close.

Again, not really my problem, though.

He's the one who ran around playing at being a force for good with the hero, despite his real job being to oversee this world.

So I ignore Güli-güli's feelings and get down to practical business.

"Detachment by way of revival has been confirmed."

"I see. How fortuitous. If the detachment had failed, we would have had to kill them again."

He looks truly relieved from the bottom of his heart.

As Hyrince, he's had a fair amount of interaction with the third prince; I'm sure he was hoping to be able to let him live.

I'm glad about it, too. It's not like I wanna go around killing people for no reason, either.

I can't say I agree with his next statement, though.

"If that's the case, perhaps we should have let him revive the king, too."

He's basically saying that he wishes we could have saved everyone.

Even though he knows that's not part of the plan.

"I know, I know. You think I am siding with them too much, yes? I have entrusted this matter to you and your side. So I have no intention of questioning your methods."

"Good."

Although you already chewed my ear off about it just a minute ago!

But fine, I'll forget about that.

Be grateful that I'm too nice for my own good.

"The elf village is next, then?"

Yep, yep.

We're on our way there now.

"Since I know you and Ariel well, I am certainly not concerned. But he has learned many tricks in his long life, too. Be ready for anything."

A word to the wise, eh?

I'm already well aware of that—don't worry.

We're gonna be fully prepared before we challenge him. There isn't chance in hell we're gonna lose.

It's just a matter of whether our casualties will be great or small.

I'm already giving this all I've got, you know.

Besides, I'm too scared of what the pontiff will do if I fail.

"Shun will be coming back soon. Excuse me."

With that, Güli-güli leaves the room.

As long as he's protecting Yamada and friends, nothing crazy will happen to them.

So I've got nothing to worry about.

I know he'd never let Yamada and the others die.

Even if they did, that man could bring them back to life if he really tried, just like I could.

The man called Hyrince is really Güli-güli's clone.

More accurately, Güli-güli transferred a portion of his soul into the still-born son of a noble in the kingdom.

The soul belongs to a god, but since the body is an ordinary human, it grew up normally and has viewable stats.

Although he can technically use some of Güli-güli's full power through that connection between souls, so if he really wanted to, he'd have the power of a god.

Since the body originally belonged to a human who had nothing to do with Güli-güli, they don't resemble each other in the slightest.

Apparently, Güli-güli has created duplicates of himself like this to act within human society from time to time.

No idea why, though.

I'm guessing he was just bored, or wanted to be all sentimental by blending in with humans, or some other irrational reason.

I mean, it's definitely not necessary for managing the world.

So it's nothing more than a game.

Of course, you can still get emotionally invested in a game.

He was best friends with Julius the hero, and they went through thick and thin together.

And then I killed Julius.

I'm sure Güli-güli must have some complicated feelings about it.

Even if he understands in theory that it was absolutely necessary.

So maybe that's why he's so hung up on Yamada.

A sort of atonement or something.

For letting his older brother die.

That's probably why he's been so overprotective that he comes and complains to me whenever I let even the tiniest thing happen to Yamada, like just now.

Speaking of human emotions, though...

Did that old man announce that he couldn't win and flee because it was his pupil's younger brother?

So even that dinosaur has those kinds of emotions, too, huh?

I see, I see.

...No, but it still doesn't really make sense, does it?

Why did he randomly show up, randomly start a fight with Yamada, and then randomly get in his feelings about it and run away?

I just don't get it.

...Seriously, what was that old man doing here?

I guess people's emotions are still just waaay over my head.

RONANDT OROZOI

The head imperial mage of the Renxandt Empire. He fought alongside the prior sword-king and became famed as humanity's strongest mage. He's also known as a master of the rare Spatial Magic. Confronted with the overwhelming power of the Nightmare of the Labyrinth, he learned his own limits and turned his focus to training apprentices.

Many have gone on to become powerful magic users, including his first apprentice, Julius the hero. On Hugo's orders, he joined the forces being sent to destroy the elves, but he harbors suspicions about the mysterious girl Sophia who accompanies Hugo.

Interlude THE PONTIFF AND THE ADMINISTRATOR SHARE A DRINK

As the evening wears late, I finish my duties and go to my room.

Since I was seated at my desk working all day, much of my body has grown stiff.

My shoulders and back ache, and while I can temporarily ease the pain with Healing Magic, there is little hope of healing it completely.

I am getting on in years.

This pain will probably accompany me for the rest of my life.

Suddenly, I find myself thinking back on all the lives I have repeated.

As I think of them, all manner of memories rise up as if they happened just yesterday.

Times that things went well.

Other times when things went poorly.

Perhaps I am becoming a little sentimental because this is the most tempestuous era I have lived through yet.

The end is drawing near, I feel.

Though I do not yet know if it will be the ending I hope for or not...

I enter my room and pick up the bottle of liquor I have been saving.

It has been a long time since I drank such things, but today, I find myself in the mood.

"Could you pour a glass for me as well?"

A voice speaks suddenly from the shadows.

Startled, I turn around to find Lord Black Dragon seated calmly on the sofa.

"...I do wish you would at least knock to alert me of your presence. Please, such surprises are not good for an old man's heart."

"That steel heart of yours wouldn't stop over something so trivial."

Lord Black Dragon smiles, unbothered by my complaints.

For someone who usually has his brow deeply furrowed in a grim expression, it is a rare sight indeed.

I oblige him by producing a second glass and sit down across from him.

Then I pour liquor into both glasses.

Silently, we raise our glasses and bring them together, touching off a clear chime that resonates in the room.

I take a small sip of liquor, and the mellow scent permeates my nose.

"This is good stuff."

"A favorite from my private stash."

I have been saving this bottle for several generations now, intending to drink it when something good happened.

Though it would be hard to claim that anything good has happened quite yet, I supposed there was no harm in opening it now.

I had a feeling that if I missed this opportunity, I would most likely be too busy to open it later.

For a while, we sit and savor the taste.

Lord Black Dragon and I are both silent, drinking only little by little.

Once we both finish our first glasses, I stand up to bring some light snacks, taking care to choose something mild enough in flavor that it will not detract from the taste of the drink.

Most people seem to prefer more flavorful snacks with their drinks, but I am sure it will not be a problem.

For a god like Lord Black Dragon, eating is a somewhat meaningless act.

In fact, though he maintains a human form, I cannot say for sure if his sense of taste is the same.

In which case, it should make no difference to him even if I simply choose whatever foods I prefer.

Especially considering that I did not even invite him here tonight.

Making such excuses to myself, I put a plate of my favorite cheeses on the table.

Looking unbothered, Lord Black Dragon reaches for the plate and helps himself.

"Oh-ho."

It seems my choice suits his tastes just fine.

As soon as he's finished with his first piece, he immediately takes another.

"You definitely have the food to match your station, Pontiff."

Evidently, Lord Black Dragon grasps the taste of human food after all.

We have known each other for many long years, and yet I only now realize that I was unaware of even this basic fact about him.

It occurs to me that we have only ever spoken of business and never once discussed our personal lives.

There was never any need.

Though I would not call him my enemy, he is certainly not my ally, either.

I am sure Lord Black Dragon feels the same way.

Though we are both working toward the common goal of saving this world, what we ultimately want to protect is different.

I wish to save humanity.

He wishes to save the Goddess.

Each of us only seeks to save the world because it is a necessary condition for saving that which we truly care about.

Saving the world is only one step in that process.

So once we accomplish that step, Lord Black Dragon and I may very well start considering very different paths.

It is that difference that prevents us from becoming allies in the truest sense of the word.

Besides, Lord Black Dragon has every right to despise me in the first place.

Because I chose to abandon the Goddess in favor of humanity.

Out of respect for that circumstance, I have never asked Lord Black Dragon for help, and I doubt he has ever entertained the idea of joining forces with me, either.

Truly, the fact that we know so little of each other's personal preferences is a perfect reflection of the surface-level relationship we have always maintained.

"I am quite fond of cheese, you see."

"Oh?"

This may very well be my last chance to have a peaceful conversation with him.

Perhaps that is why I naturally begin to speak of myself.

"It took no small amount of effort to reach this point in the cheese-making process. After the system was set up, even bacteria seemed to be affected, and all of my old methods no longer worked correctly."

"Really...?"

Lord Black Dragon looks surprised; he must not have been aware of such trivial information.

"Yes, and so I could not eat cheese for several generations. What a terrible time."

"...Now that you mention it, several kinds of liquor were lost, too."

"Indeed. Those that were already made remained intact, but it became impossible to make any more."

"Right, and so people stole it from one another for a while. How nostalgic."

It certainly is nostalgic indeed.

I imagine I would not be able to remember stories from so long ago without my Records skill.

In those days, the entire world was dramatically changed by the introduction of the system. Even I struggled not to drown in the whirlpool caused by such chaos.

Now that it is so long past, of course I look back and think I could have done better, but at the time, it was all I could do to deal with what was directly before me. Naturally, I could not stop and look at the bigger picture.

Because of that, I left my guard down and allowed the rise of the elves to occur, a terrible legacy which is now one of my greatest regrets.

Though I am loath to admit it, Potimas is a genius.

In the chaotic period after the system first began, he saw ahead farther than anyone else and dispatched his elf pawns to mingle among the humans, corrupting their minds.

This was mainly achieved by making them think the elves are their allies.

At the time, even I thought this mysterious race that had appeared out of nowhere was on our side.

They defeated monsters, quelled riots, and in time grew close to humans, often offering them help.

Since they appeared suddenly, just like the monsters, I assumed they were a sort of helpful entity made by the system's architect.

I recall a game-loving secretary who referred to them as "support characters."

"We did such horrible things to the gods, and yet they will not forsake us…," the secretary sobbed.

He believed the elves were messengers of the gods and revered them.

I wonder how he would have reacted had he learned that those elves were actually pawns of the detestable Potimas?

That man is truly the definition of wicked and cunning.

He commits acts of cruelty without hesitation.

As that thought crosses my mind, I shake my head in self-derision.

Am I myself not making plans to commit heinous acts at this very moment?

In that regard, Potimas and I are not so different.

"…We were so young back then."

As I get lost in my thoughts, Lord Black Dragon speaks to me.

As if he is reflecting on the past with both longing and regret all at once.

"Yes, indeed. Though I made an error too grave to be dismissed as youthful indiscretion."

The words escape me before I can stop them.

Even I am surprised at my own statement.

Though I kept those feelings hidden in my heart, I had never once said them aloud, and now they have slipped out on impulse.

"…Do you regret it?"

Lord Black Dragon looks at me searchingly.

After thinking for a moment, I confess the thought that I have kept buried all this time.

"Yes, of course. I always have."

I did regret it.

I knew even at the time that I was making the wrong choice.

And yet, I chose it anyway.

I chose to sacrifice the Goddess for the sake of humanity.

And since I made that decision, I have a responsibility to see it through to the end.

Even if I knew all along that it was a terrible mistake, it was my choice, and now it is my duty to fulfill it by saving humanity.

No matter what I must sacrifice to do it.

From the moment I forsook the Goddess, that was the only path left to me.

Otherwise, it would not be fair.

I cannot give up halfway through on my goal after I sacrificed the Goddess in order to accomplish it.

"I think about it time and time again. About what would have happened if I made a different choice."

I chuckle mirthlessly at myself.

No matter how much I think about it, I cannot change the past.

I am only deluding myself.

And yet, I think of it nonetheless.

If I worked together with Lord Black Dragon and Lady Ariel and the others, if we joined hands to face those trials together…

I cannot help wondering if such an absurdly convenient option ever existed.

"But there is no point in dwelling on such things now."

"Perhaps you're right."

I try to cut off my wretched delusions, but to my surprise, Lord Black Dragon responds.

"I'm the same way."

With that, he smiles wanly and tips his glass.

"I think of it all the time. Could I have done more at the time? Wasn't there any other way? A better way?"

Ah, I see.

So he has regretted it all along, too.

"But no matter how much we think about it, we'll never find an answer. That's how it is for you, too, right?"

In lieu of a response, I simply smile back in grim silence.

He's right, of course.

No matter how much I think about it, I never come up with an answer.

But at the same time, when I think it through, is it possible that this present situation is for the best? Sometimes that idea occurs to me, too.

Though I could never say such a thing to Lord Black Dragon.

How can I even think that?

Because if everything went well, then I doubt I could have ever gone this far.

It is because of that all too strong regret that I have succeeded in controlling myself and doing whatever it takes all this time.

Without it, I might very well have broken down by now.

In which case, Potimas would have only risen to even greater heights.

Despite all my faults, I do believe that I have been a successful breakwater against Potimas all this time.

If I crumbled and became useless, then Potimas would have been able to do as he pleased all the more.

That man is cautious and cowardly.

Even if I were not here, I imagine he would not have done anything truly reckless out of fear of Lord Black Dragon, but I wager things would still be vastly different without my presence.

No doubt he would have spread his influence like a slow poison, sneakily and out of Lord Black Dragon's sight.

He has always excelled at such sly, covert movements.

I know this all too well because I am the one who has contested him in the shadows all this time.

In that sense, Potimas's recent actions have been uncharacteristic.

His moves have been too big, too dramatic.

For better or for worse, there is no doubt that the foreign substance known as reincarnations has caused a great deal of movement in this world.

But even so, I feel as if Potimas's movements are rather *too* large.

I assumed it was all sparked by the reincarnations, but would that alone be enough to cause such a pathologically paranoid man to act so outrageously?

And all these movements of his have been hindered by Lady Ariel and her people, leading to several overt failures.

It is incredibly unusual for him.

That man certainly does have the rather childish habit of craving petty revenge whenever he is wronged, but even that does not explain his artless actions of late.

One might suspect that this is all part of some master plan, but his losses have been far too great.

It almost seems as if something has caused him to panic…

I do not know what the cause might be, but now the tide is shifting in our favor.

I should be happy.

When I think we might finally put that man in checkmate, I am filled with joy, a small hint of sadness, and most of all, a despondent numbness that it will all soon be over.

Perhaps this ought to be cause for celebration, but I suppose I am a bit too old.

Not just physically, but mentally.

I have been fighting for a long time. Too long. The loneliness and desolation that plagues me has long since outstripped any sense of accomplishment.

"...So Potimas will finally meet his end."

"Seems like it."

Lord Black Dragon drains the rest of his glass, looking equally full of emotion.

"I see your habit of getting off topic hasn't changed at all."

As I pour him another glass, he comments rather dryly.

At that, I realize that I have made yet another off-topic remark mid-conversation.

"Oh dear. Have I done it again?"

"I'm sure it all made perfect sense in your mind."

"...I do try my best to be careful. But it seems this bad habit is the one thing I cannot fix no matter how many times I am reborn."

I have an unfortunate tendency to get lost deep in thought and forget everything around me.

Then I speak one of my thoughts out loud without explanation, making it seem to everyone else that I have suddenly decided to change subjects, or so I am told.

Just as Lord Black Dragon says, it all seems perfectly logical in the context of my own thoughts. However, if I do not lay out all those connections aloud, it simply comes off as if I abruptly wandered off to a new topic.

"Still, if you said all of your thoughts aloud, I'm sure there wouldn't be enough time in the world."

"Very true. I imagine my voice would fail me first. Actually, I would probably bite my tongue first."

"Fair enough."

Since I am always using the Thought Acceleration skill, I can think about a vast number of things even in a short period of time.

If I tried to share everything that goes through my mind, I would have to speak terribly quickly.

In all likelihood, I would struggle to keep up and end up biting my tongue. Imagining myself doing something so foolish, I cannot help but chortle a little.

"That would tarnish your dignified image somewhat."

"Indeed. It would appear I am still better off keeping most of my thoughts to myself, even if it causes a bit of inconvenience for those around me."

With that, we exchange small smiles.

What a mysterious feeling.

I never thought I would have such a lighthearted chat with Lord Black Dragon.

But this peaceful atmosphere cannot last forever, I am afraid.

"Now, then. What business brings you here this evening?"

I know I am ruining the mood, but I must move on to the matter at hand.

"That creature's taken care of things in the Analeit Kingdom, which should alleviate some anxieties."

"I see."

By "that creature," Lord Black Dragon most likely refers to Lady White.

She is a reincarnation who has been a constant companion of Lady Ariel these past few years.

And she is also the individual responsible for changing history forever.

"Knowing her, I'm sure she accomplished everything perfectly."

"Oh-ho. You seem to think quite highly of it."

"Of course. She's the one who brought about a tidal wave of change to this perpetually stagnated world."

"A tidal wave, hmm? What an apt turn of phrase."

In all honesty, that hardly does do her justice.

Perhaps she is more like an all-consuming flood that swallows everything in its path.

A great deluge that will wash away that which has stood still in this world for so long, leaving empty land in its place.

"Potimas will meet his end at last."

I bring us back to the earlier topic.

With Lady White on the job, even someone as detestably tenacious as Potimas is surely finished.

"I wouldn't be so sure. You know Potimas as well as I do. It's entirely possible that he'll slip away somehow."

"No. I am certain of it."

There is no doubt in my mind.

Because I have fought against Potimas for so long, I know his limitations.

But I have yet to perceive Lady White's limits.

It is obvious who will prevail.

I am sure Lord Black Dragon knows this as well.

"In all probability, Lady White only sees Potimas as nothing more than just one more obstacle."

"That's true."

Lord Black Dragon agrees with my observation.

For Lady White, defeating Potimas is simply a sideshow on the way to her ultimate goal.

He is in the way of her reaching that goal, so he must be removed.

I am sure that is all she thinks of him.

And her ultimate goal is the destruction of the system itself.

"...Lord Black Dragon. Destroying the system and using that energy to revive the world... Is such a thing truly within the realm of possibility?"

Lord Black Dragon has told me about Lady White's goals and proposed methods.

I asked the same question at the time, but now I find myself asking it again.

"It should be possible, at least in theory."

And his response is the same as it was before.

Should be. In theory. It is safe to say from such uncertain phrases that Lord Black Dragon does not know for sure, either.

"The fate of the world hangs in the balance. I cannot say I am thrilled with staking everything on an uncertain gamble..."

"I know. And I haven't simply been sitting around since I first heard about it, either." Lord Black Dragon waves his hand rather irritably. "I did investigate, but I couldn't find a definitive answer. Unfortunately, I can't meddle with the system too much. Since I don't fully understand it, I don't have much choice besides relying on conjecture."

Hrm. That is sensible.

When one is trying to assess any situation, predicting the outcome requires a firm grasp of all the matters and events involved.

Without a clear understanding of the system, it is impossible to predict what results it might produce.

"But if you're willing to hear me out based on that conjecture, I do believe that reviving this world by destroying the system has a fairly high success rate."

"And your basis for that conclusion?"

"I did a rough calculation of the total amount of energy contained in the entire system and found out that it's surpassed the amount needed to restore the world. Even after removing the amount that'll be consumed in the process, I believe it should still be close to the required amount."

"'I believe.' 'Should.' It sounds to me as though this is more wishful thinking than anything else."

"None of this is a sure thing. Either way, if the attempt fails, it won't be due to insufficient energy. I'm certain about that much, at least."

If that is based on the calculations of Lord Black Dragon himself, I suppose I can trust it...

"But even ignoring objective facts, I have reasons to believe that creature has already found conclusive evidence, which might be answer enough."

"By which you mean...?"

"The thing's already discovered a method for doing exactly that. Moreover, it actually exists as an official feature of the system."

At that, my thoughts come to a halt for just a moment.

The system already has such a function?

Does that mean that the self-destruction of the system itself was always meant to be an option?

"That shouldn't be so surprising. The system has plenty of other functions that even I don't know about. Who's to say a feature like that doesn't exist?"

I suppose that is true, but to think that an option like self-destruction would be included as a regular option from the very beginning...

It makes me doubt the sanity of the system's creator.

"Besides, the system itself is already irrational in so many ways. At this point, one or two more bizarre features hardly makes a difference."

"...You have a point."

I do not wish to speak ill of the system that keeps us all alive, but it certainly is strange that it is built upon a foundation that forces its inhabitants to kill one another and then recovering energy from those who are killed.

"I suspect that it may have some connection to the Rulers."

"What do you mean...?"

A Ruler is a particular individual who has a Seven Heavenly Virtues skill, like my Temperance, or a Seven Deadly Sins skill, like Lady Ariel's Gluttony. One holder of each skill is given ruler authority.

Simply acquiring the skill is not enough to make one a Ruler; the authority to rule must first be established before any individual can become a Ruler.

Rulers receive several benefits, including permission to interfere with the system to some small degree.

"But there is no such thing included within the rights granted to a Ruler, is there?"

I am a Ruler myself.

This means I am very familiar with the authorities of a Ruler.

To my knowledge, that does not include anything to do with the destruction of the system.

"What if one Ruler alone wasn't enough? What if, for instance, all of the Rulers had to gather together and perform specific actions in a particular location?"

I cannot say for sure that such a thing does not exist.

The Rulers have virtually never cooperated on anything.

After all, three of them are in a perpetually antagonistic relationship.

Lady Ariel, Potimas, and myself.

As for the rest, they have seldom even been born.

The only time the Rulers of all fourteen Heavenly Virtues and Deadly Sins have ever existed all at once must have been at the very beginning, when the system was first put into place.

Even then, they existed in different factions, not as one united front.

In other words, the Rulers have never once assembled in pursuit of a common goal.

If there was some special condition related to such an unknown scenario, we would have no way of knowing.

As far as the particular location, I do have one inkling.

The innermost part of the Great Elroe Labyrinth.

The center of the labyrinth that the very first Ruler of Sloth spent an entire lifetime creating.

If there was such a place, it would have to be there.

"These past few years, that creature has been frantically trying to make people pick up ruler skills."

"How curious."

I had no idea.

If that is the case, then perhaps there is something to Lord Black Dragon's prediction after all.

"But if so, then would defeating Potimas not be counterproductive?"

Potimas is a Ruler, too.

If all the Rulers are required, that would unfortunately include his participation.

"I'm sure it has taken that into account and most likely formulated a strategy accordingly. Though I do not know what that strategy might be. Either way, even if we let Potimas live, there's no way he would cooperate with our plans."

"I see. If he is only going to hinder her goals, then I suppose she wants to be rid of him as soon as possible."

Potimas would never cooperate on something like this.

That being the case, then it would indeed be more effective to simply remove him and seek another approach than waste time attempting to convince him.

"But if that is truly the case, then the next target for elimination must be yours truly, correct?"

I say it in a joking manner, but I suspect it is not entirely inaccurate.

That is one scenario which I have been contemplating since before speaking with Lord Black Dragon today.

After Potimas, who is the next person Lady Ariel would find most loathsome?

That would be me. Of that I have little doubt.

What's more, the Word of God religion is weaker than it has ever been.

We lost many soldiers in the battle against the ancient mechanical weapons that were resurrected about a decade ago.

During that incident, when I temporarily joined forces with Lady Ariel and even Potimas, the Church's army was left in shambles.

I have managed to restore its strength a fair bit in the years since, but the hole has not been entirely filled.

We lost many promising young soldiers who should have built up experience and become seasoned veterans by now.

Now, since we have so few soldiers left from that era, I have been depending on old soldiers who should have long since retired and young ones too inexperienced for their posts.

But that, too, fell apart in this most recent war.

I knew from the beginning that we would not prevail, but it would have been strange if the Word of God religion did not provide any reinforcements. I had to send a considerable number of soldiers to aid the empire, none of whom returned.

Events have conspired to greatly weaken the military strength of the Word of God church, although I do think there is little point in attempting to compete with Lady Ariel on that front.

And between the announcement of a false hero and the imperial army's call for a new expedition, I am already at the end of my rope.

None of the other nations know about the false hero just yet, but if and when it is discovered, the Church will lose a great deal of influence.

That is how important the existence of the hero is to humanity.

And if anyone found out that the imperial army we allowed to pass through human lands was actually composed of demons, this religion would be finished.

It was all necessary for the sake of defeating Potimas, but if Lady Ariel also made this proposition in order to lessen the power of the Word of God religion at the same time, then her ultimate goal is likely to take my head.

That said, I agreed to all of Lady Ariel's demands, despite knowing exactly where it might lead.

"...And you're all right with that?"

"Quite. This is the perfect use of the Word of God religion at this moment. I cannot afford to miss the opportunity to ride the tides of change in this world simply because I balked at the price."

Right now, the world is changing in a major way.

The Word of God religion will be swept along with those changes, like it or not.

This current is already far too strong for the Church to resist.

So there is nothing left but to hasten it on its way.

Even if that means the Church will be dragged down by the current and crushed.

The Word of God religion exists solely to protect humanity.

If it can accomplish that goal by perishing for the greater good, that, too, is perfectly acceptable.

"For the sake of humanity. For the era of upheaval that no doubt awaits after Potimas meets his doom. The Church will become the villain against which humanity unites. I have already made the preparations."

What is required for people to band together?

An easily identifiable villain.

Anger, grief, feelings of helplessness.

And a target they can aim those feelings at.

For the masses, the belief that they are in the right is the swiftest path toward unification.

And so I will turn the Word of God religion into a villain to unite humanity.

"...You certainly are thorough."

"I have no other choice. I am not even permitted to properly atone, you see."

Atonement? That would be far too presumptuous for one such as myself.

No, I can never atone.

Which is why I must see this through to the very end.

For humanity.

That is all I can strive for.

It is for that cause that I forsook the Goddess.

So I must now offer up everything to that cause, even if it means making an enemy of the gods.

"...I must admit, I envy that decisiveness of yours. Just a little."

"......"

From my perspective, it is you whom I find myself envying.

You who can draw closer to the Goddess's side.

But while this thought crosses my mind, I do not speak it aloud.

Lord Black Dragon has his own circumstances, his own burdens to bear.

"Neither of us can quite have our way, can we?"

"You're not wrong."

After that, we stayed up all through the night, talking of only inconsequential matters.

I believe we both knew that this would likely be our last chance to spend a quiet evening drinking together.

Whether what Lady Ariel is attempting to do fails or succeeds, the times are about to become very turbulent indeed.

That is not a premonition, but a fact.

When the pivotal moment comes, I must do everything I can to ensure that humanity survives.

Because that is the only duty I have been permitted to uphold.

6   WATCHING OVER THE HERO'S PARTY FOR A LIVING

Once I finished my revival experiments with the third prince and pals, there was nothing left for me to do in the Analeit Kingdom.

Sure, things are still total chaos over there, but that's not really my problem.

The king is dead, the first prince is useless, the third prince is suspected of being involved in the rebellion, et cetera.

Man, talk about some messy court drama.

A no-holds-barred battle for the throne has begun!

Although I'm the one who engineered the entire thing.

Now I just need Yamada to get caught up in this whole business.

At least, that was the plan, but there's a new problem.

Ms. Oka woke up and told him that the imperial army, led by Natsume, is marching on the elf village.

Apparently, elves have some kind of Fartalk system for conveying information, like the Word of God religion.

Our worldwide purge of the elves has been going well enough, but it looks like there are still plenty we've missed.

Better make sure we wipe out every last one before we attack and destroy the elf village.

Since the Tenth Army has completed all missions within the empire and the kingdom, that'll be their next job.

I feel bad giving them more work to do right after such a busy period, but this is super important, so they'll have to deal with it.

Employee exploitation?

Look, that's just how it is in the military...I'm pretty sure.

Besides, I was already planning on sending the Tenth Army to finish hunting down all the elves before all this extra work in the empire cropped up. Really, it's just back to business as usual.

In other words, it's the pontiff's fault they're crazy busy now, not mine.

I'm innocent.

Not to mention, who do you think has to find the elves in every nation and deliver the Tenth Army members there in the first place?

I'm the busiest person of all!

This really is one exploitative workplace.

I should put in for a paid vacation.

Ah, I can just see the Demon Lord saying *nope* with a big smile.

Damn it all.

Anyway, to get back to the main subject here: Since Yamada and friends heard from Ms. Oka that the elf village is in trouble, they've decided to ditch their kingdom and go fight Natsume in person, for some reason.

Por qué?

It makes no sense to me whatsoever.

Like, what? I mean...

Sure, I see how they came up with that, I guess?

Humans and demons are at war right now, and they probably think it could be dangerous for all of humanity if they let Natsume keep doing as he pleases.

But does that really mean you should just abandon the kingdom that's falling apart in front of you to go take down Natsume?

I would think that the third prince, who's staying in the kingdom, would want to have the real hero Yamada fighting on his side.

You know, since he might have to go at it with the first prince's side.

Yeah, it might sound nice to say that the third prince has a big-picture attitude, but isn't he looking too far out and missing the trouble right under his nose at this point?

The kingdom might very well end up in a nasty civil war...

But I'm guessing Yamada isn't thinking about any of that as his brother ships him out.

When the third prince asked him to go, he was immediately like, "Of course."

He was probably just responding on the basis that he can't let Natsume get away with this or whatever, not thinking about the situation in his own kingdom.

I'd rather have Yamada stay in the kingdom, but now it totally seems like they're gonna send him right over to the elf village...

It'd probably be too weird for Hyrince to be the only one to object.

Sure enough, Hyrince keeps quiet, and it's decided unanimously: Yamada is going to the elf village.

Goddammit.

Yeah, okay, but there's no way he's gonna get to the elf village before the imperial army does...or so I foolishly thought.

But I mean, come on! I thought something like this might happen, so I did some prep work to make sure they couldn't get from Daztrudia to Kasanagara, the continent where the elf village is located.

With help from the Word of God, of course!

Whenever there's trouble, just call on the Church.

It helps when you're actually in touch with the guy in charge who can answer your prayers.

Still, it's not like I really did *that* much.

I just had them spread the word about the rebellion in the Analeit Kingdom and put bounties on Yamada and company.

Since officially, what went down in the Analeit Kingdom was that Yamada killed the king and tried to usurp the throne.

It was faster and more efficient to turn them into wanted fugitives than to go around telling everyone not to let them use teleport gates and stuff.

Teleport gates being the fastest way to get from one continent to the other.

That's also why we broke the one in Analeit Kingdom, to prevent him from using it in case he got that far.

Now that they're on the wanted list, it'll be harder for Team Yamada to move around.

Of course, it's not like security forces have photos or anything, which means the average person won't know what they look like. Still, I imagine local guards and stuff will be keeping an eye out for them.

But then the bastards went and flew on Shinohara, who has become a light wyrm.

Light wyrm?

More like flight wyrm!

...Sorry, please forgive me for existing. That was a terrible joke. I regret everything.

Even in video games, flying vehicles are the kinda thing you get toward the end of the game because they make getting around super easy.

You don't need to worry about roads and stuff, and you can fly right over obstacles like mountains.

In this world where monsters exist, most roads take a meandering route to avoid monster-infested regions, which means it takes that much longer to get anywhere.

But if you can ignore that and fly over everything, you'll get places way faster.

Basically, they're taking the shortest route possible.

Which also means they don't have to stop at many towns and villages, which lowers the risk of them getting caught.

They certainly haven't been caught once yet.

This is bad news, folks.

My calculations were based on them traveling by foot, but at the rate they're moving by air, they might actually make it?

...No, no, of course they won't!

I mean, don't you know where they're headed? The Great! Elroe! Labyrinth!

Obviously, they can't fly inside the labyrinth, so they'll definitely have to slow down.

Plus, the Great Elroe Labyrinth is insanely massive and complicated to boot.

If you get lost, it's practically impossible to find your way out.

There's even a labyrinth guide profession.

We've already positioned soldiers at the entrance to the Great Elroe Labyrinth.

And I made sure all the labyrinth guides know about what happened in the Analeit Kingdom and the bounty on Yamada and friends.

So they shouldn't be able to find a guide.

Trying to navigate the Great Elroe Labyrinth without a guide is practically suicide.

I should know, since I lived there for so long.

No doubt about it.

Otherwise, what are they gonna do, fly over the ocean?

I think that'd be suicide, too.

The ocean is teeming with water dragons.

Now that Shinohara's evolved into a light wyrm, I'm sure she could take a water dragon or two, but I doubt she'd be able to fend them off nonstop while also carrying everyone on a long-distance flight.

You'd have to fly all day and night with no idea when a dragon might shoot at you from the ocean, you know?

She doesn't have the physical nor the mental stamina for that.

Which means the adventures of Team Yamada end here...

Y'know, since either path would be suicide and all.

I'm sure Hyrince will stop them if they try to do anything like that.

Hopefully, they'll just kill time on Daztrudia from here on out.

...Or so I thought, like an idiot.

One of my clones is currently following Yamada's party in secret.

Guess where they are? In the Great Elroe Labyrinth.

Come on, *why?!*

They managed to get a labyrinth guide with shocking ease, totally ignored the main exit that's being closely guarded by the empire, and waltzed right on in through a secret entrance at the bottom of the ocean.

Gimme a break here!

The guide Yamada and friends found is this silver fox named Basgath.

He looks kinda familiar?

Yeah, turns out he's the very first human who found me when I was a little spider.

For some reason, he was essentially bragging to them about how he ran away from me back in the day.

And this old labyrinth guide with the explosive-sounding name is apparently the father of someone who guided Hyrince a long time ago, which is how he ended up agreeing to guide Yamada's group this time.

Um, hello? Hyrince?

Now they've got a super-skilled guide thanks to you!

What are you gonna do about it?!

Man, this guy is really good, too.

I pop into the Great Elroe Labyrinth every once in a while to check in on my spider babies, and I'll admit I end up spying on the humans in there and stuff while I'm at it.

If there's one thing I've learned in the process, it's that there are good guides and bad guides.

Even experienced guides get their paths mixed up sometimes, y'know?

And yet, this old guy is expertly leading them through the labyrinth without even glancing at a map. Only the most exceptional guides can manage stuff like that.

This guy really is a veteran, just like he appears to be.

So now Team Yamada's journey is going way too smoothly.

They've all got relatively high stats, too, which makes their pace even faster.

This is really, really bad!

At this rate, they'll make it through the Great Elroe Labyrinth with time to spare.

The only way into the elf village is by using one of the elves' hidden teleport gates, but if they use the closest one to the Great Elroe Labyrinth exit that I know of, they'll get there before the imperial army is scheduled to arrive.

Oh, by the way, I'm pretty sure I know about all of the elves' teleport gates.

My mini-mes are the best at gathering information!

I mean, they're palm-sized spiders that aren't easily detected. Unless you're specifically keeping a close eye out for them, they're incredibly hard to spot.

And I've got them scattered across the world by the thousands, making my own super-powerful information network.

Anyway, I always keep an extra-close eye on elves, so it was easy to locate their teleport gates just by tailing the sneaky ones with my spy clones.

They have to go in and out once in a while, after all.

So I think I know about all the teleport gates that have been used since I sent out my clones, at the very least.

Although if there are any that haven't been used in a long time, I wouldn't have any way of finding those.

Heh. The elves probably think we don't know where their teleport gates are.

Heh-heh-heh. Idiots.

They probably mock us, thinking we're the stupid ones who don't know anything, but now they're about to get a taste of their own medicine.

Pfft. Bwa-ha-ha!

Okay, this is no time to be making fun of the elves.

What am I gonna do about Yamada and friends?

At this rate, if things keep going smoothly, they're gonna make it to the elf village on time.

Hmm.

Should I sic the baby army on them?

I'm mostly talking about a bunch of white spiders that my old Parallel Minds produced.

Basically, they used the Egg-Laying skill to mass-produce a bunch of spider spawn.

…Except they somehow wound up attacking some human town with the Parallel Minds, and I ended up teleporting the survivors back into the Great Elroe Labyrinth here.

Ever since then, they've apparently been doing their own thing in the Labyrinth.

I popped in to say hi after I turned into a god, and they got super clingy.

I guess they still recognize me as their parent even after my deification.

Although technically, it was my Parallel Minds who made 'em, not me…

Anyway, from what I hear, folks call the baby army Nightmare's Vestiges.

Oh, and I'm called the Nightmare of the Labyrinth.

Since they're spider monsters that appeared after the Nightmare vanished, people must've just assumed there was some connection there.

Which is fair, since there totally is.

Maybe I could send the spider babies after Team Yamada to buy some time… No, wait…maybe not. Yamada and friends would totally get killed.

Even just one of those babies nearly took down the previous hero, Julius…

It's not like Yamada is significantly stronger than Julius was, so if he had to fight a whole swarm of those things, his party would get wiped out for sure.

I do think that Yamada's stats are probably higher than Julius's were, but he's got waaay less actual experience in battle.

Not as solid in the spirit and determination department, either.

So in practice, he's about as strong as Julius the hero at best, or possibly even weaker.

Julius did manage to defeat that queen taratect clone, after all.

Although, that being said, with his level of strength, he really shouldn't have been able to beat that thing in theory...but he totally did.

That hidden hero power is scary.

And since Yamada has that crazy Divine Protection skill on top of being the hero, I've gotta be extra careful.

Hmm. Hmmmm.

Seriously, what should I do, though?

It'd be kinda difficult to hinder Yamada and company without actually killing them.

We'd have to slow them down somehow while keeping everyone alive, y'know?

Killing them would be so much simpler.

But I won't do that, because Ms. Oka is with them, of course.

Still, even if we managed to just injure them a bit, a little Healing Magic would fix it up right away, and that would be that.

It wouldn't even slow them down.

Should I just straight-up teleport them back to the kingdom?

...Nope, that's no good.

I don't have enough hands to spare.

Honestly, I'm so damn busy right now that I don't really have time to go personally mess around with Yamada and friends.

The best I can do is send someone else to try something, but my only option in the Great Elroe Labyrinth is the spider-baby army.

And if I give those kiddos an order, I can easily see them getting too excited and going overboard.

Even when one of them attacked Julius the hero, it was because they somehow learned that I was planning to take him down in the war, and they wanted to take care of it for me ahead of schedule.

If I asked them to slow down Yamada and company, I could totally see them doing something totally horrifying like cutting off their legs.

Or worse, just getting carried away and killing them outright.

If they killed anyone besides Yamada, he could bring them back to life, but it's one hundred percent still too dangerous. Better not risk it.

Honestly, I'm way too busy to deal with this right now. Since I can't do much to them anyway, it's probably for the best if I just don't bother trying to interfere.

I don't have time to waste on them, quite frankly.

Even just keeping an eye on them like this is about the most I can do.

Still, I gotta admit, it's actually pretty fun to watch them.

What's fun about it, you ask?

Oh, you know. All sorts of things.

I never get bored, that's for sure.

They always run into one crazy situation after another when I'm watching them.

Like Shinohara turning into a human.

Or the time it turned out that she totally couldn't swim.

Man, that Humanification thing was a shocker.

I went through sooo much trouble to become an arachne, and here she is, turning into a human just like *that*!

Even after evolving into an arachne, I had to turn into a damn god to get a fully human form, you know!

And there was no Humanification skill on my list of options, either!

It's no fair that dragons get to do that by default!

If dragon monsters get it, spiders should get it, too!

Except unlike dragons and wyrms, spiders don't have universal skills like that!

But whatever. It's fine.

Especially since, after all that, everyone found out Shinohara can't swim, which must've been sooo embarrassing for her.

Psh. I can't believe that stuck-up bully couldn't even swim.

You think I could see that without laughing?

Nope, not possible!

Aaah-ha-ha-ha-ha!

I can't help taking a bit of pleasure in her suffering, probably because I have memories of being bullied by her.

Although the person who was actually bullied is the real Hiiro Wakaba, also known as D.

And I'd imagine it was probably more like being barked at by a harmless little puppy from D's point of view.

But since the memories feel unpleasant to me, I guess D didn't exactly enjoy it, either.

I assume.

Anyway, then the helpless non-swimmer Shinohara got chased in the water by a water dragon, just flailing around like an idiot.

Ahh, that was fun all right.

And then the dragon's breath attack sent her flying, messed up her swimsuit, and got Yamada a nice little fanservice event, too, which was all hilarious to boot.

Shinohara doesn't really seem to be aware of Yamada as a guy, but since she got squished up against him in such an unladylike state, of course he ended up staring at her a little.

What is this, a rom-com?

Obviously, there's gonna be a bunch more accidental romantic moments after this, and she's totally gonna end up falling for Yamada...

Then it'll develop into a love triangle, and *bam*, we've got a juicy soap opera on our hands!

Oh man. Is Yamada gonna get stabbed to death, or will it be one of the girls? I'm on the edge of my seat here.

No, wait a sec.

Considering the effects of Yamada's Divine Protection skill, isn't it more likely that things will stay on the romcom route and somehow build up to a harem ending?

What a scandalous skill! I'm definitely not jealous!

If every girl who joins Yamada's side ends up falling in love with him, that skill is even scarier than I thought!

And it really does seem like a high percentage of them have already fallen head over heels.

Like his little sister, right? And Hasebe? And Ooshima?

Shinohara's not there yet, and I don't think Ms. Oka feels that way.

I don't really think that half elf erstwhile maid of his, Anna, is in love with him, either.

It's kinda more like loyalty than love, if I had to describe it?

Although I guess you could argue an oath of loyalty is pretty closely related to a declaration of love.

The nuance is just a little different.

…Huh?

I was only joking, but is it just me, or does Yamada actually have a harem forming around him?

Although that's on hold right now thanks to Natsume.

…How much of this is the effect of the Divine Protection skill, I wonder?

If they fell for Yamada because of his personal virtues, that's all well and good, but it'd be kinda messed up if it was because of a skill.

See, this is why it's so hard to plan around a skill when you don't know its exact effects.

What if that lucky-lecher moment when they got blown away by the water dragon was due to Divine Protection, too?

But if that's the case, wouldn't it mean that deep down, Yamada is secretly hoping for events like that to happen…?

W-well, he is at that age, I guess…

All jokes aside, though, it's definitely kinda heartwarming to watch Team Yamada's adventures.

I guess you could say there's not much of a tragic tone to any of it.

Lately, everyone I have to do with seems to have some level of desperation due to a tragic backstory of some kind, y'know?

There's the ones who try to fight against the grim fate of the demon race, like Agner, Balto, Warkis…

Not to mention the pontiff, who created a whole religion just to protect humanity and has been working his butt off basically forever.

Plus, there's Black, who's basically stuck between several rocks and hard places.

And of course, the Demon Lord, who rose up to save the Goddess.

Every last one of them has been driven to the depths of despair, and yet they keep fighting back without ever giving up.

It's painful to watch.

But Yamada and friends don't have that air of tragedy.

Sure, they've been through a lot themselves, and it's not like they're taking this lightly.

But still, they're just kinda lacking it somehow.

The determination.

I guess that's probably because they haven't gotten into one of those situations yet that really puts your determination to the test.

Julius the hero, on the other hand, chose his own path in no small part because he had his determination constantly called into question.

But since this crew hasn't experienced what I would call true suffering yet, it still doesn't feel like they've really got their feet on the ground.

Not that you'd really want to get used to a violent, hack-and-slash world like this one, I guess.

But this is the same world Julius the hero wanted to protect.

So even though I'm sure these guys are totally serious, I can't help getting a kinda warm and fuzzy feeling when I watch over them.

Watching guys like Agner was just stressful, and I ended up having to personally send him to his death, so that didn't help.

…But if Yamada and his merry band do reach the elf village, they're definitely gonna get caught up in the impending storm.

I doubt things will stay heartwarming for them then.

Because if they get involved in the battle at the elf village, they're gonna find out just how awful this world truly is.

I was really hoping they would just sit tight and behave until it's all over, without having to learn any of that.

But if the journey is going this smoothly for them, it means that's what Yamada himself really wants.

At this point, I definitely have to suspect that Divine Protection is at play here.

And if this is what Yamada wants, if they're going to get there no matter what's waiting up ahead, then they'll just have to accept whatever happens there.

Even if it's something that goes against Yamada's wishes.

Thus, we had some laughs, a few tears, and a little bit of sentimental rambling, to the point where I want to make fun of myself for going on such an emotional rollercoaster, but the long and short of it is: Sure, I'm keeping an eye on Yamada and friends.

It seems like Hyrince doesn't want them to get to the elf village so quickly, either, as he appears to have planned an obstacle of his own.

As soon as Team Yamada sets foot in the Great Elroe Labyrinth, the craziest thing shows up.

An earth dragon, to be specific.

It's a freshly evolved one, so weak that it doesn't even compare to Araba.

I guess he had a wyrm in the Upper Stratum quickly exterminate a bunch of monsters up there so it could level up and evolve.

Man, way to mess up the whole ecosystem. Again.

I roll my eyes as I watch Yamada's party do battle.

A dragon is still a dragon, even if it's a relatively weak one.

Its stats and skills are far beyond those of any ordinary monster.

Even Julius never defeated a dragon. (Although I bet he could have taken on a lesser dragon if he encountered one.)

But for Yamada and company, this thing is far and away the strongest monster they've ever encountered.

Incidentally, if you don't worry about categories like monsters and stuff, the strongest foe Yamada has ever faced is our own Vampy.

She'd be able to defeat an earth dragon like that without even breaking a sweat.

In other words, if they can't even take on a baby earth dragon like this one, they definitely won't be able to beat Vampy.

Still, Yamada's stats are high enough that he's probably not gonna lose, even if he might struggle a little.

Plus, it's not like he's alone—he's got allies like Shinohara.

Now that she's evolved into a light wyrm, Shinohara's stats are even higher than Yamada's.

Monsters' stats seem to go up faster than humans', just like mine did back in the day.

Even though she's technically still a wyrm, it looks like Shinohara's stats are on par with a full-fledged dragon.

See? Just now, she sent that earth dragon flying.

Imagine a dragon getting punched in the face by a little girl and going down hard...

I mean, can you blame me for thinking it looks a little pathetic?

It looks like I'm not the only one who thinks that was embarrassing: The earth dragon itself is practically steaming and charges at Shinohara in a rage.

But Shinohara easily blocks the swipe of its claws.

So much for the pride of earth dragons...

After that, they use some kind of firestorm magic to pin the earth dragon, and Yamada delivers the finishing blow. Just like that, the earth dragon is done for.

Farewell, sweet pride...

Wow. Never mind slowing them down, didn't you basically just give Yamada some EXP *and* the Dragon Slayer title on a silver platter?

Ahh, maybe that's what Hyrince was after in the first place.

Like, if it doesn't seem like we can stop him, we might as well make him a little stronger?

Hmm. Well, there's no way of knowing right now what Hyrince was really thinking, but this totally worked out in Yamada's favor.

Divine Protection doing its thing again, maybe...?

At this point, I'm incredibly tempted to just blame every stroke of luck Yamada comes by on his Divine Protection skill.

Wait, what's this now?

"Hero?"

Making a surprise guest appearance while talking to Yamada and friends by way of Telepathy is one of my spider babies.

Huh? What are you guys doing here?

Um, hang on a sec, I don't want you to do anything weird...

Crap. I've kinda got my hands full at the moment, so if the baby army decides to attack Team Yamada, I can't stop them.

What do I do?!

"Hero." "Ruler?"

"Ruler." "Ruler." "Ruler." "Ruler." "Ruler." "Ruler."

Oh geez, a whole bunch of babies are swarming around them now!

"Cannot be Appraised?"

"Cannot be Appraised." "Cannot be Appraised." "Cannot be Appraised." "Cannot be Appraised." "Cannot be Appraised." "Cannot be Appraised."

"Ruler?"

"Ruler." "Ruler." "Ruler." "Ruler." "Ruler." "Ruler."

"Reincarnation?"

"Reincarnation." "Reincarnation." "Reincarnation." "Reincarnation." "Reincarnation." "Reincarnation."

"But they're weak?"

"Weak." "Weak." "Weak." "Weak." "Weak." "Weak."

"Weak. Weak." "Weak. Weak." "Weak. Weak." "Weak. Weak." "Weak. Weak." "Weak. Weak."

Hey now! Just because they're weak doesn't mean you can attack them!

"You know about reincarnations?!"

There goes Yamada.

Is this guy totally fearless or what?!

I can't believe he's actually talking to the spider-baby army.

He's not worried they'll attack him?

"We do." "We do." "Of course we do."

"Why do you know that?"

Phew. It doesn't seem like they're gonna jump him right away, at least.

"Master." "Master."

"Mother." "Mother."

Okay, you're talking about me, right?

"Is this 'Master' a reincarnation?"

"You'll know soon enough." "You'll find out soon enough." "You'll find out." "You'll know."

Yeah, I guess that's true.

If Yamada and friends end up reaching the elf village, we'll probably meet face-to-face.

"What do you mean?"

"Proclamation." "Pronouncement."

"The beginning of the end."

"The world begins."

"The world ends."

"Please wait! What does that mean?!"

Yeah, seriously, what *does* that mean?!

Do these kids even know what they're saying?

They're not just trying to sound cool and foreboding for no reason, are they?

"You don't need to know."

"You'll die anyway."

"You'll all die."

"Just struggle to survive."

With that, the babies disappear, leaving Yamada and his party alone.

Ugh, now what…?

Looks like my kids are going through an edgy phase right now…

Now that they made it out of sight of Yamada and company, they're jumping around looking super pleased with themselves, like *We did the thing!*

Where did I go wrong raising you guys?

…Well, they didn't attack him, so I guess it's fine.

They just rattled off some needlessly cryptic BS and freaked out Yamada and his friends… What were they trying to accomplish, exactly?

I have no idea what they're thinking, even though they're basically my descendants.

Was it a warning or something?

I dunno, though. I don't think that'll help.

At this point, it sorta feels like nothing Yamada and his friends do is gonna matter. They're in so far over their heads.

In a way, I guess the babies might have succeeded in getting their group a little more mentally prepared for the worst.

Does that mean this was technically a positive event for Yamada, too?

…I dunno.

Divine Protection isn't all-powerful; I probably shouldn't blame it for every little thing.

If it *was* omnipotent, Natsume's plot wouldn't have succeeded in the first place, for one.

Plus his sister and Hasebe are still in Natsume's clutches…

There's no harm in being extra cautious, but I guess I shouldn't be overly paranoid, either.

For now, I'll just keep watching over Team Yamada.

Interlude   THE HERO'S SISTER, THE EVIL GOD'S PUPPET, AND THE HUNTING DOG

I look down on the world from the window.

Below, I see the imperial army dispersing, heading to the rooms they've been assigned.

Among them, I recognize the face of the sainthood candidate Yuri and scowl despite myself.

"Hey there. You're looking grouchy as usual, my dear fiancée."

The door to my room opens without so much as a knock, and Hugo peers in.

"Silence, false hero."

"Ooh, very scary."

Looking unconcerned, he enters the room and throws himself down on the sofa.

"And don't call me your fiancée. Disgusting."

"Damn, that's cold. Fine then, Sue."

"Don't call me Sue, either. Only my dear brother and my closest friends are allowed to call me that."

"Yeah, yeah. Princess Suresia, then."

Hugo shrugs while flashing a nasty grin.

Just looking at him turns my stomach, so I direct my gaze back to the window.

The imperial army is steadily approaching the elf village.

The troops will be resting here for today, then using a teleport gate tomorrow to move on to the next location.

And this room has been assigned to Hugo and me.

The two of us are technically engaged to be married, though it is very much against my will.

Most likely, this arrangement is only to make it seem natural for he and I to be seen working together.

But even if it is only a farce, the idea of being engaged to this man makes me want to vomit.

I would kill him right now were it not for the sake of my brother.

Yes, all of this is entirely for my beloved elder brother's sake.

So I must endure, no matter how awful it may be.

One day, I met an evil god.

Despite her pure-white appearance, she was utterly evil.

When I went to punish the sinful fool named Hugo for attempting to harm my brother, delivering judgment with my own hands, I found that evil god doing *something* to Hugo instead.

My instincts told me that I couldn't beat her.

If I tried to defy her, I would die.

As I stood frozen in true fear for the first time in my life, the evil god whispered to me.

"Shall I spare your big brother from any harm?"

From that moment on, I was in thrall to that god.

She promised that so long as I followed her orders, she wouldn't lay a hand on my brother.

For his sake, I swear I'll overcome any trial…

"We'll be at the elf village pretty soon."

Even without looking, I can tell Hugo is smirking.

He usually is, even though there's nothing funny about the situation.

"Heh-heh. I can't wait."

I wish he would simply be silent and stop fouling my ears.

If my elder brother's voice is like a symphony from the heavens, this man's is like a grating performance on rusted strings.

Oh, how I wish I could hear my brother's voice now…

Even a few scant words would ease the fraying edges of my heart…

"I hope you don't mind if I join you."

Ugh.

Another pest has arrived.

"Hello there, little princess."

This is the evil god's underling, Sophia Keren.

"What do you want?"

"I came to see how you're doing, of course."

"Then you've already seen, have you not? So please go away."

It's bad enough that I already have to put up with Hugo, the unbearable eyesore. If I'm made to endure any more, I might go mad with the stress.

"My, how rude. Couldn't we at least chat a little?"

"I have nothing to say to the likes of you."

"Oh, I see. And here I thought I would comfort the poor, tearful little girl who pretended to be brainwashed and betrayed her precious big brother."

"Why, you…! That's none of your concern! You're just a god's faithful hound!"

I wasn't pretending—I really was brainwashed that time!

For some reason, probably by order of the evil god, I had no control over my body when I killed my father.

Why would she do such a thing?

This is just a guess, but I think she might have been giving me a way out.

So that it wasn't my fault—I was just brainwashed.

That evil god is crafty and merciless, yet sometimes, she shows some half-hearted kindness.

Honestly, it would be easier for me to understand if she was simply pure evil through and through…

"Oh, am I? But aren't you in the same boat now? That's why you betrayed your brother."

"No! I would never betray my brother!"

That is the one line I will never cross!

"But you *are* obeying our master, regardless. That makes you an enemy of humanity."

"Nnngh!"

"There we go. Now *that's* the face I wanted to see."

Sophia's lips curl with pleasure.

"You're the worst."

"I'll take that as a compliment."

What an awful person.

She might even be eviler than the evil god herself.

I wish she would just die…

"Oi, Sophia. You're not even gonna say hi?"

"Oh? I didn't realize you were here."

Sophia glares at Hugo as if she were looking at a parasite.

"Don't make that face. I've got feelings, too, y'know?"

"Oh, do you?"

And what's wrong with looking at a worm like a worm?

My eyes might rot out of my head, having to take in a worm and a she-devil at the same time.

"Well? Have you managed to get one of the Seven Deadly Sins or Seven Heavenly Virtues skills yet, princess?"

"…No, not yet."

"Well, that's a shame. Have you forgotten your promise to Master?"

Nnngh.

I did make a promise with that evil god.

I said I would help her and that I would acquire one of the Seven Deadly Sins or Seven Heavenly Virtues skills.

If I can accomplish that, she'll guarantee my brother's freedom and set me free.

But I haven't managed to do it yet.

"Well, I suppose it doesn't matter much. I don't think Master had very high hopes for you anyway."

"Ha! Guess some of us are just built different."

I clench my fist.

How humiliating!

I can't bear to be looked down on by such filth!

"That face is even better." Sophia's smirk widens. "A spoiled little princess who grew up wanting for nothing, trembling in humiliation. Now that's a sight for sore eyes."

Scum. The absolute lowest of the low.

"……"

See, even a massive scumbag like Hugo looks taken aback.

Why should scum that alarms even other scum deserve to live?

I wish they would die…

Aside from my brother, what's the point in all the riffraff that persists in this world?

I wish everyone but my brother and I would just die.

"But is the plan still gonna work if this one doesn't make it in time?"

"It should be fine. It seems the more ruler skills that are acquired, the better, but I'm told that the bare minimum has already been met. I imagine it will just be easier if there are more, no?"

"Uhhh, sure. Not that I care, 'cause I don't really know how to use the ruler skills'…keys, was it? Whatever."

I don't see how he can be so carefree when he's being controlled by an evil god and evidently has two of these "keys."

As far as I know, they have a total of six keys so far: Hugo's Greed and Lust, Sophia's Envy, and a few I haven't met, namely someone called Wrath with the corresponding skill, someone named Merazophis with Perseverance, and the Demon Lord Ariel's Gluttony.

I don't know what these keys are for, either.

But I doubt the evil god is going to use them for anything decent.

"Isn't it more of a problem that Yuri can't get one? She's a reincarnation just like us, dammit."

"I'm sure some are suited to it better than others, even among reincarnations."

I almost feel bad for Yuri, too.

Even if she was a rotten harlot of a nun who kept trying to seduce my brother, it's cruel that she's been brainwashed and forced to do their evil bidding…

But I suppose I don't really care, since she tried to tempt my brother and all.

Maybe she'll just screw up and go off to be with that god she loves so much.

Since she's a true believer and all, I assume she would like that.

"Oh, that reminds me. I heard your dear brother is heading to the elf village. Did you know?"

"?!"

My brother?!

"Maybe you'll get to have a touching reunion there."

Brother…

I want to see him.

But I'm also afraid.

What am I going to say to him…?

"I'm told Ms. Oka is with him, too. Not to mention Katia, Fei, Anna…he's very popular with the ladies, isn't he?"

Those harpies…

I see now.

While I've been suffering like this, they've been cozying up to my beloved brother…

I was always suspicious of that "Ms. Oka" woman.

And then there's Katia.

I thought she was a friend, but if she dares touch my brother, I won't show any mercy…

"Y'know…this chick's quick to trash-talk other people, but she's just as bad, isn't she? There's no way she's thinking anything good or wholesome right now, am I wrong?"

"Master would never take a truly decent person under her wing, obviously. She picks and chooses so that she won't feel too bad if they have to suffer a little bit."

"Heh, gotcha. Makes sense to me."

The scumbags are talking among themselves now, but it's just the incoherent warbling of garbage masquerading as people.

I won't pay them any mind.

7 SUMMING THINGS UP AND PLANNING WHAT COMES NEXT FOR A LIVING

Considering how freakishly busy I've been lately, you gotta wonder why I didn't take care of more of this stuff before everything hit the fan, right?

Well, let me clear that up right now!

I didn't have time!

I was really busy before, too, even if it wasn't quite this bad!

After all, I am technically a commander.

I had to manage my troops and all that stuff.

And guess what?

On top of that, my core force is the Tenth Army, which barely had any soldiers to its name.

I had to gather up the losers who didn't even fit in the leftover divisions, forming the Tenth Army out of a bunch of problem children who couldn't find a home anywhere else, you know?

How long do you think it took to break...I mean, train them into real soldiers, get them armed, and wrangle them into the bare minimum level of functionality for an army?

Day in and day out, I spent every second preparing them for battle without a moment to rest.

Talk about exploitative.

I demand! A paid vacation!

Ah, I got denied again...

And guess what *else*?

I was doing a bunch of other stuff at the same time, too.

First of all, improving on my mini-mes.

You know, the information-gathering clones I unveiled during the big war.

Basically, I took the palm-sized spider clones I created initially and made them stronger.

They're still the same size, but they're stealthier, immune to any detection skills, and can even transmit everything they see and hear right back to me.

I expanded on that feature even more during the war so that they can now transmit those images to special monitors, too.

They're like super-efficient self-driving mega-cameras!

I scattered thousands of them all over the planet, using them to gather all kinds of information in real time.

That's how I got the deets on where all the elves are at, too.

Not to mention their hidden teleport gates.

Heh-heh.

The Word of God religion and the elves are both pretty keen on information gathering, but none of them hold a candle to meeee!

That said, these little spy clones have zero firepower and can easily be crushed by a stray footstep, which is a bit of a bummer.

That doesn't happen super often, since they're so stealthy and all, but once in a while, there are accidents and stuff like that.

But I guess we'll just have to call that the cost of doing sneaky business.

Even if it *is* a major pain to replace them when they get squished.

So I was simultaneously operating a few thousand spy-ders while doing all this, right? And that's while producing a bunch of battle clones at the same time.

As you might imagine, battle clones are mini-mes that are meant to be used for fighting instead of spying.

Unlike the spy clones, they come in different shapes and sizes depending on their purpose.

First, we've got the mass-produced all-purpose battle clones!

These guys are about three feet in size.

They look more or less like me in my Zana Horowa days, the form I evolved into right before arachne.

Basically, a white body with scythes for the two front legs.

And they're just about as strong as I was back then, too.

They shoot lots of magic—I guess it's technically conjuring now—they use Evil Eyes like crazy, and they counter with the scythes if an enemy gets too close.

They're fully loaded with thread and poison, too, of course.

As you can gather from the fact that I called them mass-produced, I've got lots of these all-purpose battle clones.

How many? Well, that's a military secret.

Next up is the queen taratect clones.

That's what I sent in against Julius the hero during that war.

They're clones I made based on Mother, the "bigger boat"-level huge ones, that crush things with the sheer power of their giant bodies.

Honestly, their overall capabilities aren't that much higher than the all-purpose battle clones.

But since they're physically so much bigger, they cost a lot more to make, which means I've only created a handful.

Finally, there's my aces in the hole: the space-specialist clones.

As the name implies, they specialize in spatial conjuring. They're the same palm-sized shape and appearance as the spy clones, but their abilities are on an entirely different level.

They can create other dimensions, erode the fabric of space—crazy stuff like that.

Since becoming a god, I've developed an incredibly high aptitude for spatial conjuring for whatever reason, and these clones are loaded up with the culmination of all that progress.

They can slice through space to remove heads and whatever else. Without some way of countering that, no enemy stands a chance against these space-specialist clones.

I mean, they could teleport your torso right off the rest of your body.

Even if you try to run away, they can tamper with space itself, so there's nowhere to go.

The only way to counter them would be by meddling even further with my spatial meddling; you'd have to be at least as good at it, and probably better.

In system terms, I think even maxing out Dimensional Magic, the evolved form of Spatial Magic, wouldn't be enough to save you.

In other words, it's basically impossible to oppose me for anyone who operates within the bounds of the system.

Damn, I'm strong. Waaay too strong.

These battle clones generally exist in a separate dimension created by the space-specialist clones.

I can call them out whenever I need them.

Although at the moment, the only time they've seen any outside action is when I sent a Queen clone against Julius the hero.

I'm not slacking off; I'm just putting them into power-saving mode to conserve energy.

Don't get the wrong idea there.

When Vampy and company defeated those legendary-class monsters and such, I fed 'em to the clones in my separate dimension, saved up some energy, and created more clones whenever the energy stores went past a certain point.

I've been slowly but surely increasing the numbers of my battle clones with that routine.

Considering that they started as cute but useless palm-sized spiders, they've come a long way, that's for sure.

Seriously, those things were absolutely worthless at first.

Slow and steady wins the race, I guess.

Not everything is like skills, where you're guaranteed to get stronger if you keep training, but I think you're still bound to get a certain level of results if you put in lots of hard work.

Anyway, I've got one more kind of clones, a pretty weird type.

These ones are very much related to a different job I've been working on in addition to my job as a commander.

These clones are called system-related clones.

I assume you can piece that one together.

Basically, these clones have various tasks related to the system.

My ultimate goal is to destroy the system and use the energy released to rejuvenate this world.

There's a lot of thorough preparation involved, as you might imagine.

And to do all that preparation, I'll need to understand the workings of the system down to the tiniest detail.

This is a make-or-break gamble with the fate of the world on the line, after all.

You can't be too careful, even to the point that it might seem borderline paranoid.

So even in the early stages, I've put a ton of extra work into investigating the system.

Between my job as a commander and all that clone work, I was seriously busy for sure. But honestly, it's this system investigation that's taken up the bulk of my resources.

The fact that I created clones for this specific purpose should tell you just how much effort I've been putting into this.

To sum it up, I've had no time to rest whatsoever!

Do you get it now, people?

Even before things got as busy as they are now, I was still crazy slammed!

Who among us would dare go up to that super-busy spider of the past and tell her, *Hey, things are gonna get even busier soon, so put your back into it?!*

Even if I did know the future, I would've said, *Sorry, I'm already at my limit!*

Come on, Labor Standards Act, do your thing here!

Ah, this is a different world, which means that doesn't exist here…riiiight…

This suuucks.

But I'm still gonna do it, since I'm the one who decided to take all this on in the first place!

So let me give you the rundown on what we've learned about the system so far.

First of all, what exactly *is* the system?

Well, it's a super-huge conjuring created by D!

Its main purpose is to dole out skills and stats and stuff to all the living things in this world, collect all of that in the form of energy when those living things die, and use that energy to revive this dying world!

Damn, that's a long sentence!

Where's the TL;DR?!

And that's still simplifying it quite a bit, just so you know.

Basically, the system is a messed-up conjuring that forces anything living in this world to save up energy while they're alive, then pay it all back when they die like some sick loan shark coming for their due.

Training your skills and stats is the main method of saving up that energy, a gamelike feature which I think is probably D's personal preference.

And that energy is used to help restore this world, which is on the brink of destruction.

If you're wondering why the whole world has to depend on such a convoluted system in the first place, it's because the humans of this planet really screwed things up long ago, apparently.

If you wanna know the details about that part, ask Taboo.

It even comes with a free service where you get to hear a voice saying "atone" all the time, whether you're asleep or awake.

Although I weaseled out of that little contract when I became a god!

It was always pretty annoying, so that was a relief.

Anyway, enough about Taboo. From what I'm told, the people of long ago managed to use up this world's energy until it was almost completely drained. Then this goddess became a sacrifice to fill that void.

I don't really know the details myself.

Honestly, I don't think I really need to know, either.

I'm guessing that knowing more about it would just make me sick to my stomach.

After spending time with people who were there when it happened—like Black, the pontiff, and especially the Demon Lord—I've definitely gotten the impression that some awful stuff went down.

And since the living things in this world are trapped in a hellish cycle where they die, get their energy stripped away, and are reborn into the same world all over again, I suspect that's intended as a punishment, too.

Although I wish they wouldn't drag us Earth reincarnations into their problems!

Back to the subject of the system, though. Aside from those basic functions, D also added a solid handful of just-for-fun features.

That includes most of the gamelike aspects, like skills and monsters.

I don't think stuff like skills, stats, levels, and so on were really necessary to get living things to store up energy.

That part definitely smells like D messing around to me.

What about monsters, you ask? That's a little harder to define.

Even if the initial idea of skills and stuff was just for fun, once you've chosen that as the method for saving up energy, you need to have everyone fight one another.

Monsters were created to give people something to fight.

If this is a video game, they're the enemy characters.

And the system generated those enemies.

But I get the impression that the system only created monsters at the beginning, and they've been naturally reproducing on their own since then.

Since it costs energy to produce monsters, it's better for the system's purposes if the monsters breed anyway.

Ultimately, this means the monsters that currently exist are a mix of various factors: descendants of the monsters initially created by the system, animals that already existed in this world that adapted to the current environment, and some combination therein, to the point where you can't even categorize them all anymore.

At this point, all the system really does with monsters is imprint them with the instinct to attack humans on sight.

I know that sounds like a massive pain from the humans' point of view, but it's not like there's an obvious alternative if the system needs living things to fight one another.

Besides, monsters are an integral part of the food chain at this point. It'd be worse for the world if they suddenly disappeared.

In addition to monsters, the system has other ways to make people fight one another.

Namely, the hero and the Demon Lord.

The hero is human.

The Demon Lord, a demon.

They each lead their respective peoples and fight each other.

Both of them get titles with unusual perks and abilities, too.

The hero gets the special effect of being able to match the demon lord and can use the Sword of the Hero. Plus, the hero can power up in a crisis.

While the demon lord doesn't have a special effect against the hero, they can use the Sword of the Demon Lord.

It seems like a bit of favoritism toward the hero, but that's because humans and demons have different base specs and life spans and such; it's basically a handicap because the demon lord is likely to end up stronger than the hero.

Without that, humanity could easily end up at the mercy of one demon lord for ages.

The problem here is that with the hero's special effect against the demon lord, he can fight on equal footing no matter how much stronger the demon lord might be.

Except that means that for a weaker hero to catch up to a strong demon lord, a bunch of energy has to come from somewhere.

So basically, the anti-demon-lord effect is really a power-up that steals energy from other parts of the system.

And did I mention the current Demon Lord is the strongest in history?

Like, her stats hover around 100,000 on average.

What would happen if the hero tried to fight her?

A huge amount of energy would be pulled out of the system and totally wasted, that's what.

We can't splurge like that when we're trying to save up energy here!

Besides, this whole thing also means that the existence of the hero is a threat to the Demon Lord's safety, which is why I obliterated Julius during the war and hacked the system to try to remove the very existence of the hero feature while I was at it.

As we all know, that ended in a big fat failure.

I researched the system pretty thoroughly and thought I'd be able to pull it off, but I guess that was overly optimistic.

But I learned my lesson, which is why I'm now trying to deepen my understanding and control of the system even more.

And what I really need for that control is the ruler skills.

We're talking about the Seven Deadly Sins skills and the Seven Heavenly Virtues skills.

These skills actually serve as keys to access the system.

Once you have a ruler skill and you establish your ruler authority using the information obtained from Taboo, you get a bunch of special privileges.

Like the abilities to block Appraisal, do a search of the system itself, and so on.

Still, using those special privileges too often will wear down your soul, so I can't say I recommend abusing them—except blocking Appraisal, which doesn't seem to really cost anything.

The ability to block Appraisal came in handy quite a few times before I became a god.

Anyway, while I was investigating the system, I figured out that you can use these ruler skills as keys to access a sort of secret menu.

When you get your ruler authority confirmed, a list of things you can do is basically installed in your head, but this was most definitely not on that list.

In other words, you'd have no way of knowing about it unless you've thoroughly inspected the system like I have.

So I did all that and found out about the secret menu.

And wouldn't you know it...

It contained the system's self-destruct program.

Just as I suspected, given the awful nature of D's personality, of course she would include a hidden backdoor.

It even comes with a nice little README file explaining how to use it. You gotta laugh.

Makes you wonder if there was any point slowly saving up energy through the official menu in the first place.

And if I felt that way, I'm sure it was even worse for the likes of the Demon Lord and the pontiff, who really have been slowly, carefully saving for all these years...

But luckily, since the Demon Lord was on the verge of giving up, she was thrilled to see some light at the end of the tunnel at last.

Although I'm sure she wishes she'd known about this method sooner.

I mean, if they'd activated this right after the system was created, the world could've been saved already.

They wouldn't have had to suffer through this long, drawn-out cycle of living, dying, and passing on energy through the official channels.

I'm sure there have been more tragedies throughout history than you could count, and the Demon Lord and the pontiff have probably seen all of them.

So I imagine learning that those might not have needed to happen in the first place must've been tough.

But you can't change the past, so I guess there's no point dwelling on it.

I can't alter the tragedies that have already taken place. I can only try to make a better future.

Let time travelers handle past crises, although I don't know if anyone even exists who can manage something like that.

I mean, D has a crazy amount of knowledge—I wouldn't be surprised if she could do it.

If nothing else, though, I certainly can't.

I've gotta focus on what I *can* do instead of dwelling on what I can't.

But wait!

There's one thing I can't do by myself!

And that's increasing the amount of people with ruler skills.

Ruler skills are the keys to the system.

See, you actually need all the ruler skill keys to activate the self-destruct program in the system's secret menu.

Every! Single! Key!

Yep, that does it. This game is impossible!

There are several ruler skills that aren't even held by anyone right now.

Worse yet, one of the people who *does* have a ruler skill is someone who will absolutely never cooperate with us.

You guessed it: Potimas.

Honestly! Why does that guy have to get in our way at every turn?!

The dude's very existence is a thorn in my side!

Do you have any idea how I felt when I figured out how to activate this secret menu?!

I wanted to run right into a wall!

But it's just like that famous basketball coach once said: "If you give up, the game's already over."

I racked my brains over what I could possibly do, and in the end, I decided to cheat.

Keys, doors, opening...

Yeah, let's pick the lock!

...You there, the reader who just thought *What the hell does that mean?*

If the direct approach doesn't work, you've just gotta use workarounds instead!

Since this secret menu itself is already a workaround, there's nothing wrong with using yet another workaround on it, if you ask me!

Besides, I've got no other choice, because I'll never be able to get the keys from all the ruler skill holders otherwise.

At any rate, I sat down and made a list of people who might be able to get ruler skills.

Then I decided to recruit as many as I could.

We already started with three people with ruler skills on our side: the Demon Lord has Gluttony, Vampy has Envy, and Mr. Oni has Wrath.

Next, I began conducting close surveillance on demon army commanders, famous humans, fellow reincarnations, and other important characters.

My spy clones definitely came in handy there.

And next thing you know, Mera picked up the Perseverance skill.

That was a bit of a shocker.

Mera was originally just a normal person, you know?

He's had a pretty wild ride of life since then, especially since he turned into a vampire and all, but I still can't believe he came so far as to get a ruler skill.

It's supposed to be suuuper hard to get those skills, you know.

I mean, even Julius the hero didn't have one!

If even the appointed defender of humanity couldn't get any, that's definitely a rare set of skills.

…Although I guess I can't really talk, since I had four of them, or five if you count Wisdom.

By the way, it seems like the Wisdom skill was made specifically for me.

I got it when I maxed out Appraisal and Detection, but the Demon Lord's done the same thing, and she didn't end up with Wisdom.

Oops, I'm getting off topic.

At any rate, Mera really worked hard.

Good work, Mera.

Keep it up, please.

Perseverance is the key here.

Show me what an ordinary human can really do.

Although I guess he's a vampire, not a human anymore.

Meanwhile, on the human side, Natsume really screwed things up.

He tried to plot an assassination to get revenge on Yamada.

Although it ended in failure thanks to Ms. Oka.

On top of that, she even used her ruler authority to erase all Natsume's skills.

Since Ms. Oka was able to use those Ruling Class Privileges, that means she has a ruler skill.

And she's even established her authority.

There's no way Ms. Oka has maxed out her Taboo skill, so Potimas must have told her how to do that. I'm sure he has his authority established, too, naturally.

Most likely, Ms. Oka's ruler skill is Charity, one of the Seven Heavenly Virtues.

I used to have that one, too.

I got it when I was saving tons of people's lives; it just randomly came with one of the titles I got.

It's unclear whether Ms. Oka got it in the same way or if she used skill points to acquire it.

But how she got the skill isn't that important, as long as she has it.

As long as Potimas is around, though, I can't really go near her.

So if Ms. Oka has a ruler skill, that also means there's one less key that I'll be able to use.

That hurts, for sure.

But there's nothing I can do there.

It was always going to be impossible to get all the keys anyway.

Man, though, Ms. Oka really overdid it.

Out of all the ruler privileges, erasing skills eats up an especially large portion of your soul.

Normally, that should have done some serious damage to her soul, enough that she could've lost a bunch of skills and had her stats seriously lowered in the process, too.

Ironically, it might be thanks to Potimas that Ms. Oka came out unscathed.

Part of Potimas's soul is attached to her like a parasite.

Actually, that's true of all elves, not just Ms. Oka.

I think this is an effect of Potimas's Seven Heavenly Virtues skill, Diligence.

He can take over people he's infected and use them as his own body doubles.

Once someone's been taken over once, they can never go back to their old selves.

In other words, Potimas was basically holding Ms. Oka hostage.

Note the past tense, though.

That was before the Natsume-goes-crazy incident.

Ms. Oka used her ruler privileges in a way that should have consumed her soul, but miraculously, it consumed the soul of Potimas that was parasitically infecting her instead.

I don't think even Potimas saw this coming.

Thanks to that, the part of Potimas's soul that was attached to Ms. Oka got seriously weakened, making it much harder for him to take over her body.

All that being said, it's only harder, not absolutely impossible, which is still concerning.

But still, anytime Potimas is inconvenienced, I've gotta celebrate!

Besides, that wasn't even the only advantage we gained from this little incident.

We also succeeded in brainwa—I mean recruiting Natsume to our side.

Hmm? Was I about to say *brainwashing*?

No, you're imagining things.

There's no such thing as the brainwashing clones that I conveniently didn't mention earlier.

And there's definitely not a fingertip-sized spider inside of Natsume's brain or anything like that! What is this, a horror movie?

Ha-ha-ha.

Look, if we just left him alone, he definitely would've gone crazy again and gotten himself executed this time for sure. So why shouldn't I use him to our advantage instead?

And then I really hit the jackpot: He gained not one but two ruler skills, Lust *and* Greed!

Talk about a bargain.

We've pulled off all kinds of mischief thanks to Lust's brainwashing effects, so now I can say for sure that I made the right choice!

Although I wasn't expecting Yamada's little sister to attack while we were brainwa—I mean *persuading* Natsume.

Gotta admit, the thought of keeping her quiet through violent means did cross my mind for a second—but when you really think about it, she's actually pretty smart and talented, enough that she did a respectable job holding her own alongside a reincarnation like Yamada.

Doesn't that mean she stands a chance of getting a ruler skill?

That's why I very kindly approached her to suggest that she work with me in exchange for not doing any harm to Yamada.

Since she's a little *too* obsessed with her brother, that threat—no, wait, I mean *offer*, definitely just an offer—worked on her right away.

Unfortunately, she hasn't been able to get a ruler skill just yet.

But considering that she still helped us out with some other small favors, I've kept my promise not to do any harm to Yamada.

With my own hands, at least!

I never promised that Natsume wouldn't hurt him, okay?

And I've still made sure that he stays alive, okay?

So I haven't broken my promise.

Anyway, all jokes aside, I am planning on making sure she doesn't get caught up in the shock waves that'll inevitably come when we destroy the system, as thanks for helping us out.

Especially since I did kinda make her kill her own father.

I did have Natsume brainwash her and force her to do it, to make sure it was against her will at least, but it might've still been a teensy bit traumatic for her.

Next, I used Natsume's brainwashing abilities to control other reincarnations like Ooshima and Hasebe and check whether they had any ruler skills.

If they did, I was planning to steal the keys from them while they were still brainwashed, but sadly, none of them had any.

I didn't brainwash Yamada, since I made a promise to his sister and all.

Not to mention the little matter of Divine Protection.

I'll admit, part of it was that I was just scared something weird would happen if I tried anything on him.

The fact that Yamada turned out to have the Mercy skill definitely stings, though.

Maybe I should've broken my promise to his little sister and stolen the key from him...

Well, no use crying over spilled milk.

And Shinohara is usually attached to Yamada at the hip, which means I can't touch her, either.

So that's the deal with the reincarnations at the human academy.

Other than those guys, there's also Tagawa and Kushitani, two other reincarnations who've been traveling around the world as adventurers and built up a fair amount of combat experience, too.

Neither of them seems to have gained ruler skills as far as I can tell, so I've just been keeping an eye on them, but then they clashed with Mera in the war and ended up following Ms. Oka to the stupid elf village.

Maybe I could have stopped them if I tried, but it would've seemed weird for us to intervene at the time, and I was so busy with cleanup afterward that I just ignored 'em.

There's also a reincarnation named Kusama who's been working under the pontiff, but he doesn't have a ruler skill, either, placing him solidly in the ignore column.

Hmm? I'm dismissing Kusama way too easily?

It's not my fault. He's just that kinda guy.

The other reincarnations are all confined in the elf village, and I seriously doubt they'd be able to get ruler skills in that situation, meaning they also get ignored.

To sum it up, the current ruler skill holders are as follows:

Wrath: Mr. Oni.

Envy: Vampy.

Greed and Lust: Natsume.

Gluttony: Demon Lord.

Pride and Sloth: Both unclaimed.

Mercy: Yamada.

Perseverance: Mera.

Diligence: Potimas.

Charity: Ms. Oka.

Temperance: The pontiff.

Chastity and Humility: Both unclaimed.

Of the fourteen, I've acquired the keys for six.

Four are unclaimed, and four belong to members of other factions.

I would've liked to get at least half of 'em down, but this might be the best I can do...

I'll just have to use lockpicking for the rest.

So yeah.

As far as that part goes, apparently, the difficulty varies based on the state of the ruler skill.

Specifically, in order of highest difficulty to lowest: authority established > authority not established > unclaimed.

Unclaimed skills are basically like the key is lying around undefended near the lock, but if someone has the corresponding ruler skill, it becomes a lot harder because someone else is basically carrying the key around.

And if they've also established their ruler authority, it's kinda as if there are additional security measures around the lock itself.

It's because of this range in difficulty that I was able to figure out someone already had the Mercy skill.

In other words, the hardest ones to contend with at the moment are Diligence, Temperance, and Charity.

Mercy takes fourth place.

If I can just figure out these four somehow, the unclaimed ones should be easy enough.

I'm gonna kill the crap out of Potimas soon, meaning Diligence will go back to being unclaimed.

So I'll just wait to pry it open until after all that.

As for Charity, I might be able to talk Ms. Oka into handing over the key once Potimas is good and dead.

I don't know if she's going to agree or not, but if I have a chance of resolving it peacefully, I might as well wait until then.

Which means that one's also on hold until I massacre Potimas.

I'm not sure if there's much I can do about Temperance…

Let's just put that one aside for now.

I can make a judgment call on it after I kill Potimas.

That leaves Mercy as the highest priority.

It'd definitely be best to pick that lock before Yamada establishes his authority.

Once he maxes out his Taboo, it'd be great if he decided to help us… But if not, then it's gonna be a huge pain.

Prying it open before then would be safer for sure.

Same goes for the four unclaimed ones.

I held out for as long as I could, but I doubt any of my players are gonna pick up a ruler skill anytime soon at this point, even if I put it off a little longer.

If anything, the chances might be higher of someone on a different team getting one instead.

Even among the people on our side who might get one, there's an all-too-real chance that they might lose their lives in the battle at the elf village.

That even goes for the ones who already have a ruler skill, like Vampy and Mr. Oni.

And if they die, then another Ruler seat will be empty again.

Better to at least use the keys that I already have now and open as many locks as I can before any of that happens.

"So yeah, I'm gonna go take care of that stuff real quick."

"Hmm. You can't let those 'system-related clones' of yours take care of it like usual?"

I report in to the Demon Lord before I head out, since communication is important.

We're in a horse-drawn—or rather *spider-drawn*—carriage.

It's basically a fancy basket being carried on the backs of arch taratects. The lap of luxury.

"Nope. It'd be too risky for me to control them remotely from afar for such an important job."

"Gotcha…"

I can understand why the Demon Lord would want me to hold off, though.

We're right in the middle of preparing for battle with Potimas, which is clearly very important to her.

I can gather information on the enemy faster than basically anyone else in the world, I can teleport anywhere at any time, and I can even deploy whole formations that way. Since I'm the strongest force on our side, it's no wonder she'd want to keep me close at hand.

Huh?! Wait, I'm so skilled it's scary!

Is it just me, or am I too talented for my own good?!

Is this even allowed?

I'm not gonna get banned for hacking, am I?

I'm just that talented. It's almost creepy.

"White...you're lost in some stupid thoughts again, aren't you...?"

"I don't know what you're talking about."

"I'm pretty sure you only say that when I've hit the nail on the head."

"I don't know what you're talking about..."

The Demon Lord rolls her eyes and shrugs exaggeratedly.

Grrr. Offense taken!

And I want to file a complaint against the super-toxic work environment in the demon army, too!

As the CEO, the Demon Lord should pay me a settlement!

"......"

For some reason, the Demon Lord grabs my hand tightly and pulls me toward her.

Whaaa—?

As I freeze in place, she lays me down and promptly bundles me up in her own thread.

The thread is woven like cotton and wrapped around my entire body.

Um, whaaa—?

"You can take care of that tomorrow. For tonight, you sleep right here."

Sleep?

In this bundled-up state?

Okay, I'll admit that this is actually super soft and comfy, but still.

If I sleep bundled up adorably in the Demon Lord's carriage, what about my dignity?

"White, do you even realize how exhausted you look right now?"

"For real?"

Is it that obvious?

I guess I have been working too much overtime lately.

Even though I'm a god, I still have a physical body that can get tired.

Maybe I've been pushing it a little too much.

"But there's not much time..."

"It'd be worse if you doze off and mess something up."

Fair!

They say that since your performance gets worse when you're tired, it's actually more effective overall if you take regular breaks while working.

"All right, then."

"Good. Have all your clones and stuff rest, too, except for what's absolutely necessary."

"Oh c'monnn…"

But then my whole worldwide surveillance network will temporarily shut down…

"Well? I'm waiting."

"…Fine."

Sheesh, the Demon Lord's kinda pushy today.

Seems like she's gonna force me to sleep by any means necessary.

"…I am aware that I've been relying on you too much, you know."

"Hmm?"

The Demon Lord murmurs something with a bit of a rueful expression.

"So when I see you looking this exhausted…well…you know. I want you to rest, that's all."

"…I'm doing it because I want to, okay? Don't make that face."

"Sorry. No, wait. I guess what I should be saying right now is thank you."

"Yeah, exactly."

"Once it's all over, I really want to thank you again, properly this time. So don't fall out on me before then, okay?"

"You got it, boss."

In that case, I guess it's time to sleep!

I'm gonna get drunk on sleep!

Goodnight!

Special Chapter   A GRANDMA ADMIRES HER PROGENY'S HARD WORK

Within moments, White is snoozing quietly.

It's been a long time since I saw her sleeping so defenselessly.

In fact, she hardly ever sleeps this deeply at all.

The only time I remember is after she became a god, when she lost her powers.

Even then, she was heavily on guard at first and would wake up right away at the slightest sound or movement.

But then either she came to trust us more, or perhaps she decided there was no point being on her guard since she had no powers left anyway; at any rate, she started to sleep more soundly.

When she was staying in the duke's mansion in the demon territory, she apparently slept like a log.

But there was much less of that once she started getting her powers back.

And I think she completely stopped letting anyone else see her sleep right around the time she resolved to destroy the system and save the world.

Ever since then, White has been running nonstop.

Even though I know all she really wants to do is laze around…

Watching her reminds me of the original Ruler of Sloth.

A Ruler who loved lazing around but kept working nonstop until it eventually killed them.

At the time, I couldn't do anything to help.

Because I was much weaker than I am now.

No, that's not right. Even now, I'm depending on White far too much, hardly doing anything myself.

In the end, I still exist inside the system.

There's not much I can do when it comes to what goes on outside it.

The most I can contribute is to force White to sleep like this.

It frustrates me to no end.

I want to help her more.

In fact, the reality is even more painful. White is originally an outsider here, and we're forcing her to take on all these burdens.

It's not just White, either.

Sophia, Wrath...

Even Merazophis, though he's not a reincarnation.

They're all generously lending me their strength.

I really do feel fortunate.

Maybe even as much as those days when I was surrounded by the first Rulers, or even more.

Back then, I was just a weakling, being protected by all of them.

But it's different now.

I've gotten stronger.

Strong enough to fight, to defeat Potimas.

I can't help White.

But I'll do everything within my power until I'm spent.

It's the least I can do to repay everyone for helping me.

I'll express my ultimate gratitude by seeing it through to the end and making sure it all succeeds.

Lady Sariel.

The first Rulers, who have long since passed on.

Please watch over me.

I'm going to save this world with my own two hands.

I promise.

And then, if possible, I want to celebrate with White and the others.

So please, White.

Don't push yourself too hard, okay?

8 PICKING A FIGHT WITH THE SYSTEM FOR A LIVING

Aah, this is so nice and comfy.

I slept well, all right.

Now I'm nice and refreshed.

"Good morning."

"Morning."

I crawl out of the fluffy bundle.

"Mm'kay, this time I'm going for real."

"Right. Oh, but first, take this."

Hmm?

The Demon Lord hands me something.

"…Huh?"

"You need that, right?"

Yes, the object she handed me is definitely something I need.

"Thanks. That's a big help."

"Don't worry about it. You're the one who's helping *me* out."

But this will definitely make my job a lot easier.

"This is pretty much the most I can do…"

…You really don't need to worry about *that*, you know.

After all, the reason I decided to save this world in the first place is the Demon Lord herself.

"All right, I'll be back soon."

"Okay, have a safe trip. Be careful."

…That exchange almost made us sound like a family.

Aw, I'm a little embarrassed.

I quickly teleport away to hide my embarrassment.

When I reappear, it's in a very strange space indeed.

This is the center of the system.

A giant conjuring circle forms complex geometric patterns all across the floor.

It even spreads over the walls and ceiling, glowing with a faint, fantastical light.

And in the center is a woman, the lower half of her body gone as if she's melting into space, suspended in midair as though the conjuring circle is binding her there.

The Goddess Sariel.

The core of the system, the sacrifice who was offered up to this world, and the precious person whom the Demon Lord called Mother.

<Proficiency has reached the required level.>

<Experience has reached the required level.>

<Proficiency has reached the required level.>

And although the Goddess's lips aren't moving, a cacophony of her voice echoes and overlaps endlessly in this room.

The system messages that the Word of God religion regards as the voice of god.

Coming to this place makes me incredibly uncomfortable.

Why? Well, every single sight in this room is disturbing, that's why.

Maybe it's because it shows just how selfish the humans of the past really were, or maybe it's that even though the Demon Lord adores her and wants to save her so desperately, the Goddess herself doesn't share that wish.

"……"

I shake my head lightly to dismiss those thoughts.

Throughout the mysterious room, there are small white spiders here and there.

Those are my system-related clones, and they're already on standby.

There are fourteen distinctive conjuring circles that stand out in the room, distributed around the Goddess at the center.

Those are the keyholes.

I can open them by inserting the corresponding keys.

First, I'll open the seven locks that I already have keys for.

There's the six I already had and the seventh that the Demon Lord gave me before I left.

Since I'm opening these properly, there's no problem so far.

This next part will be the real challenge.

I move the system-related clones to make contact with the conjuring circles that correspond to the unclaimed ruler skills.

The lockpicking is about to begin.

But then a sharp voice interrupts.

"Irregularity detected."

Unlike the overlapping voices that have been echoing this whole time, that clearly came out of the Goddess's mouth.

"Outside interference confirmed. Activating defense mechanism."

…Yeah, that's about what I expected.

Power gathers around the Goddess.

That's the defense mechanism or whatever getting ready to shoot.

Well, I'm basically breaking and entering here, after all.

It's no surprise that there would be a home security system in place.

Honestly, I knew this would happen.

Especially since I've already set off this defense mechanism once before.

It was during the war, when I tried to abolish the hero function.

The defense mechanism went off just like this, and the clones that were trying to modify the system were physically destroyed.

As a result, I failed to get rid of the function of the hero, and Yamada of all people was chosen as the new one.

Since the system-related clones aren't made for fighting, this is one job they can't handle.

Clusters of energy form around the Goddess, taking on shadowy forms.

They become pitch-black silhouettes, just barely taking the shape of humans.

There's twelve people in total.

Or would you even call these people?

"Commence elimination."

As my idle thoughts meander in a stupid direction, the Goddess gives an order, and the shadows all move at once.

They're headed right toward me—and whoa, they're so fast?!

Just as I take a quick step to the side, a fist flies past my face with a gust of wind.

One of the shadowy figures closed in on me insanely fast and nearly landed a punch right on my nose.

Damn, that was fast!

Wicked fast!

Yiiikes!

Whew, that scared me.

Maybe I wasn't being careful enough.

Since I've gotten so good with my god powers, I might've been a little overconfident.

How could I come that close to getting hit by such an obvious Telephone Punch?

Wait, another one?!

The same shadow is charging at me again.

It's basically just swinging wildly, no polish or technique whatsoever.

But with that unbelievable speed, it's still a pretty serious threat!

That said, it's coming in a straight line, so it'll be simple to dodge.

I sidestep the telegraphed attack and avoid it again.

After the shadow passes, a loud *boom* follows.

The sound came after—does that mean it's moving faster than the speed of sound?!

Are these shadows even faster than the Demon Lord, if nothing else?

As I wonder about this, an invisible blade flies toward me.

Whoops, looks like they're not just speedy after all.

Wait, is this thread?!

The weapons moving toward me are threads, too fine for the naked eye to see.

There's ten of them in total.

It looks like one of the shadows shot out threads from each of its fingers and is manipulating them.

Heh. So you think you can take me on in a battle of thread?!

Time for you to learn your place!

I'll turn the tables on you in no time!

So I shoot out ten threads from my own fingers as well, countering the shadow's attack.

Bwa-ha-ha! You think those feeble threads can reach my feet—whoa, whaaa—?!

We're actually evenly matched!

But how?!

You're telling me there's a thread user who can fight on equal footing with me?!

Our threads *crack* against each other like whips, whirling and feinting at each other with pulls and twists as we try to cut through each other's threads.

It's an incredibly close contest.

And then the speed shadow charges toward me!

I put my fight with the thread shadow on hold to get some distance between us.

Then another shadow suddenly appears behind me.

When did you get there?!

With no time to turn around, I just shoot a Black Spear at it from my back.

It doesn't exactly look awesome, but I can produce conjurings from anywhere on my body!

The shadow that was trying to pull off a surprise attack on me is getting a surprise attack of its own!

Or so I thought—but then it disappears just as suddenly as it arrived.

This time, I sense its presence carefully and figure out how it's *poofing* around!

The shadow is turning its body into a mist form to make it look like it's disappeared.

Sure enough, the mist concentrates and reverts to a shadow.

What's up with that vampire-like ability?!

Vampy can do that kinda thing, too, right?! Although she and Mera never really use it!

And now more threaaad?!

The thread surrounds me completely, boxing me in.

Retreat! Teleport!

I escape with a Short-Range Teleport.

Phew. Now I can get my—wait, wha—?!

A speed shadow just grazed me?!

Hang on, time out!

Gimme a second here!

Spatial Separation!

I cut off the space all around me, creating a cube-shaped void barrier.

Since the entire space is separated, no physical or magical attacks can pass through.

You'd have to be on my level of spatial conjuring expertise to get in from the outside.

In other words, it's practically invincible.

The only downside is that it blocks out all light and sound, too, meaning I can't tell what's going around outside, either.

At any rate, this will protect me from enemy attacks.

I'll take that moment to calm down a little.

Okay, so the defense mechanism shadows are way stronger than I expected.

Maybe I was being careless or overconfident or whatever, but even then, isn't it awfully strange that they were able to corner me like this?

I am a god, remember?

In terms of abilities, I'm pretty sure I'm way stronger than I ever was as an arachne…

Now, my current strength is spatial conjuring. In terms of stats, I would probably still fall short of the Demon Lord, I think.

Even then, I would estimate that I've got the equivalent of stats in the 50,000 or 60,000 range.

So what the heck does it mean if I still can barely keep up with these things?

It's like I'm fighting a whole bunch of Demon Lord–tier opponents.

Nah, I guess they're probably individually weaker than the Demon Lord, but still.

Maybe Vampy or Mr. Oni would be a better comparison?

Yeah, that seems about right.

And a dozen of them, no less…

On top of that, thus far, I've only been able to confirm the abilities of three of them: the speed shadow, the thread shadow, and the mist shadow.

I don't even know what the other nine do yet.

Considering how unique the first three have been, I seriously doubt the remaining nine are just generic mass-produced fighters.

It's probably best to assume they've got some crazy abilities, too.

I guess I should've expected no less of the defense mechanism protecting the system itself.

This isn't a hopeless situation by a long shot, but it's gonna be tougher than I was expecting, that's for sure.

All right!

I've calmed down a little.

Let's give this another shot.

...First of all, it'd be dangerous to just deactivate the barrier right now. Instead, I'll teleport somewhere directly outside of the barrier.

All at once, I'm free from the soundless, pitch-dark space.

And the first thing I see is, yeesh, a whole big swarm of...somethings.

There are so many black-silhouette creatures that you can't even see the Spatial Separation box I was inside a moment ago.

Um, I'm pretty sure those weren't there before...

Where did these things come from...?

Oh, never mind. I see the source right there.

One of the human-shaped shadows is producing a bunch of monsters.

That guy over there's clearly the culprit.

Is it just gonna keep churning out endless mobs if I don't stop it...?

Guess I better take that one down fast.

Ah, but first...

I produce a Spatial Separation wall right in front of me.

Then the speed shadow slams right into it.

If you keep trying the same attack over and over in such a short time, I'm gonna get used to it no matter how fast you are, dummy.

The speed shadow collides with the Spatial Separation wall at the height of its impressive speed and absorbs all the recoil to boot.

A normal wall would probably absorb part of the impact, but this is an actual separation in the fabric of space, not a physical wall.

If you crash into it, you're taking every bit of that impact right to the face.

The speed shadow crumples to the floor.

One down.

...Or so I thought, until a blast of light coming from another shadow hits the wounded one in the back.

The speed shadow hops right back up.

Ugh. They've got a healer, huh…?

If the healer shadow can restore the others, then I've got to crush that one, or it'll keep bringing the other shadows back.

So the summoner shadow and the healer shadow.

Those are my top priorities, but which one should I go after first?

I guess probably the healer.

There'd be no point beating the summoner shadow first if the healer shadow just brings him right back to life.

Death to healers. No mercy.

All I gotta do now is avoid the recovered speed shadow, the thread shadow, the mist shadow, the swarm of shadow beasts, and whatever else comes at me, all while targeting the healer shadow.

The speed shadow only uses simple charge attacks, and the thread shadow is actually easier to avoid if I don't try to fight it with more thread.

As long as I'm careful of the mist shadow, I can tell when it's about to appear.

I couldn't react fast enough before because I wasn't expecting it and had to fend off an attack at the same time, but the cat's out of the bag now.

As for the big swarm of beasts, they're not much to worry about.

In fact, to be totally honest, these shadows are weak.

I can even wipe them all out with some dark missiles that I conjured a bunch of as a smoke screen.

Compared to the shadows, they're practically trivial.

Although that's probably why the summoner shadow can crank them out so fast.

As soon as I wipe out one wave, there's already a bunch more. It's extremely annoying.

On top of that, they're actually working together against me pretty well.

That's probably thanks to the shadow that's standing next to the summoner shadow, pointing at me and giving orders with gestures.

Is that a command-related ability, maybe?

It might be granting them some kind of ability-enhancing buff, too.

Looks like it's giving all the shadows orders, including the beasts, which is why they're coordinating their attacks on me.

That's kind of a pain, too.

But still, the healer shadow comes first!

Avoiding the intermittent attacks from the beasts, speed shadow, and so on, I send a Dark Spear flying toward the healer shadow.

My attack hurtles at its target, but then a different shadow jumps in front of the healer and blocks it.

This one's got a shield.

I can't believe it blocked my conjuring...

Guess this shadow is fairly strong, too.

Each of them would probably have stats in the tens of thousands. Maybe they'd even be on par with legendary-class monsters?

It'd be nearly impossible to deal with a dozen of them if your strength was bound by the limits of the system, wouldn't it?

The Demon Lord might be able to take them...

No, I guess this would be tough to solo even for her, huh?

Maybe she could do it if she brought the puppet spiders and some more backup?

If it'd be this hard even for the Demon Lord, then this is normally an impossible level.

Guess that means they really don't want you to cheat.

But I'm gonna do it anyway!

The healer shadow splits in two.

I used Spatial Separation to cut it in half.

Since I'm messing with the fabric of space itself, it's physically impossible to defend against.

You'd have to be at least as good with spatial manipulation as I am, or else the only thing to do is dodge.

But I'm very confident in my spatial abilities, and there's no way to tell it's coming, making it next to impossible to sense or predict and dodge.

In other words, it's a completely unfair attack that basically insta-kills as soon as it's activated.

Now *that's* one down.

...Except I was wrong. Again.

A plump-looking shadow comes running over to the healer shadow and hits it with light.

And the healer shadow is back on its feet like nothing happened.

Oh, come on.

You can even bring 'em back from the dead?

And there's another one besides that healer shadow, too?!

I wasn't told about this!

Come on, you gotta be kidding me! Listen up, system!

I know this is the defense mechanism of the system's core, but should you really be giving these things the ability to bring the dead back to life, which is practically number one on the list of things that should be totally off limits in this world?

I mean, you can only collect energy if something dies in this world, so preventing that by resurrecting someone should be out of the question.

I won't say it's against the rules, but it one hundred percent goes against common courtesy.

And should the system itself really be so brazen about flaunting this unspoken rule? Hmmmm?

There's only one skill that can even revive the dead, and that's Yamada's Mercy.

You're totally messing up the game balance, dude.

Is this like a penalty from the moderators against a player who's broken a rule?

Should be grateful that I didn't get my account banned on the spot?

Knowing D's power, I'm sure she could impose a penalty that would instantly wipe me out if she really wanted to.

Since that didn't happen, that means she's still holding back a bit.

And if she's still holding back, then D still wants this to be a beatable challenge.

Although I'm pretty sure you seriously screwed up the difficulty level!

Or was that on purpose?

Is D demanding that I should be able to handle something this insane?

...Okay, actually, I could totally see that.

D basically said that she was bored of this world and wanted to ditch it because it was at a standstill.

In other words, the people of this world couldn't live up to D's standards.

That's an evil god for you.

Sticking them with an extreme difficulty mode, then getting bored and throwing them aside because they couldn't beat it...

Isn't that a teensy bit too selfish?

But I guess that just means she's so strong that people have to forgive her, or rather have no other choice but to let her do what she wants.

Even I'm in no position to complain.

I guess this is a real-world example of *absolute power corrupts absolutely*...

Maybe it really is D's fault that this world ended up in such a mess, huh?

Her standards were way too high, making it impossible to win...

That would certainly explain why the Demon Lord, the pontiff, and all of them were never rewarded in spite of all their hard work.

You know, thinking about this is actually starting to piss me off.

Why does the Demon Lord have to suffer because of that jerk's stupid demands?

In fact, *I'm* suffering because of it right this second!

I use Spatial Separation to cut the speed shadow in half.

But then the thread shadow, the mist shadow, and a whole bunch of beasts all charge at me, forcing me to go on the defensive.

And while I'm busy dodging, the resurrection shadow brings back the stupid speed shadow.

We've just been repeating this cycle over and over.

I've killed the speed shadow the most, but I brought down the thread shadow and the mist shadow a few times each, too.

But every single time, they just get revived.

If I kill them instantly with Spatial Separation, the resurrection shadow fixes 'em up; if I don't get a one-hit kill, the healer shadow does it instead.

I feel like I'm playing an endless game of whack-a-mole here.

It seems like the resurrection shadow is the only one that can bring back the dead, not the healer.

So if I could just take that one down, things would get a hell of a lot easier, but obviously, my enemies are all too aware of that fact.

So the other shadows have been aggressively protecting the resurrection shadow.

The shield shadow and the barrier shadow are both guarding it nonstop.

In theory, my Spatial Separation should be able to take out the target anyway, even if there are tanks in the way.

…But in practice, they've figured out a way to stop me.

How the heck are they defending against an attack that insta-kills regardless of the distance or the enemy's defenses, you ask?

It's similar in principle to the magic-neutralizing effect that dragons have.

Dragons' scales and barrier-related skills interfere with the fundamental building blocks of magic, weakening the effect of spells.

And the building part actually isn't any different for conjuring.

In theory, any skill that can block magic should also be able to hinder my conjurings.

It just happens to require a much higher output, since it's *my* conjuring that you have to stop.

I'm a former magic expert who once had the Height of Occultism skill, you know?

Even though it's conjuring now instead of magic, I'm still just as strong! …I think.

But now, my conjuring is being obstructed.

By the shield shadow and the barrier shadow.

One obviously holds a simple shield, and the other creates simple transparent barriers.

I think it's the latter that's blocking my conjurings.

But it's hard to imagine that just one of them is single-handedly negating my powers, so I'm assuming the shield shadow has some kind of obstructing effect as well.

Basically, the two of them are working together to crush my magic.

Although spatial conjuring is my area of expertise, and I can produce it without much effort, it still uses high-level, super-complex runes.

So it's not my fault that I can't break through a blockade of two stupid shadows!

At least, that's the excuse I'm going with.

In reality, spatial conjuring originates in the fabric of space by nature.

If the targeted part of space is within the range of the obstruction, the construction will fall apart as soon as it starts to activate, making it weaker to barriers than other kinds of conjuring.

You'd think I could just shoot them from afar with other kinds of conjuring, then, but that doesn't work, either.

I tried tossing some Dark Spears, but they lost most of their power as soon as they touched the barrier, then got blocked by the shield shadow and dissipated completely.

Grrr.

These guys' magic-jamming abilities are crazy strong.

They might even be on par with Vampy, no?

Thanks to her Ruler of Envy title, Vampy has a maxed-out skill called Divine Scales, the strongest of the dragons' anti-magic scale skills.

Basically, it's the strongest magic-blocking skill in existence.

As far as I can tell, the shield and barrier shadows have magic-obstructing abilities that are on par with Vampy's.

In fact, is it just me, or is the barrier maybe even stronger than hers?

Man, what a pain.

What am I supposed to do about these guys…?

Seriously, every single one of them is strong enough to take on an army alone…

How am I supposed to fight *twelve* of them…?

Now I'm really getting fed up.

So far, we've got the speed shadow, thread shadow, mist shadow, summoner shadow, commander shadow, healer shadow, resurrection shadow, shield shadow, and barrier shadow.

That's nine in total.

As for the other three: One of them has just been standing in front of the Goddess this whole time without moving.

The other two are chasing my system-related clones around.

One of them seems to have a bunch of different abilities; it's using all kinds of magic to sling attacks at my clones as they run around like crazy.

And it also seems to have telekinesis or something, because there's a bunch of different swords, axes, spears, and other weapons floating around for no discernable reason.

But the fact that they're floating there means it can probably use all of those, too.

What a multitalented bastard.

As far as the other one goes, well, I'm not really sure.

I can tell it's trying to do *something* to my clones, but they've been resisting all its attacks so far.

It looks like they're being attacked by something invisible, but I can't tell what's happening exactly.

Since they're totally resisting it anyway, I could probably just ignore it.

But considering how strong all the other shadows are, I get the feeling that if they fail to resist it at any point, it's not gonna be good news.

Although since it's targeting my clones and not me, I assume it's nothing totally insane like instant death or something.

Wait, what if it actually is, though?

Like, *what if* they're planning on taking out the weak-looking clones first.

But it's not working, sooo...

I would think it'd be more efficient to help the others fight me than to waste time chasing my clones in that case.

And just as that thought crosses my mind, the commander shadow gives some kinda gesture and sends them after me instead.

Hrm.

I couldn't tell what was hitting my clones, but if it tries it on me, maybe I can analyze it?

The mysterious shadow that was going after my clones turns toward me, and...uh, whatcha doin', bud?

It's striking some kinda weird pose.

Like, the weirdest, most indescribable pose you can imagine.

Is it trying to look cool, or...?

Since it's just a jet-black shadow, it doesn't have a face to speak of, but I can almost imagine it winking or something.

At the same time, the mystery attack it was using on the clones comes at me, too, but of course I easily resist it.

Um, okaaay...

How am I supposed to react to this?

You can't just drop some stupid comedy routine on me in the middle of this super-serious fight scene...

The shadow changes its pose.

Huh? Seriously, what am I supposed to do here?

Since another invisible attack came at the same time, the poses must have some kinda meaning, but this is kind of a lot...

Uhhh, I guess I'll try analyzing the mystery attack?

I take a peek at the nature of the invisible attacks the mystery shadow has been sending at me.

...Ahh, I get it.

It's some kind of charm attack.

The type that's supposed to make the target do your bidding.

Which means those poses really are meant to look cool...

I guess they're supposed to enhance the charm effect or something.

But I'm a spider, and I'm not super interested in an interspecies romance...

Plus, I'm a god, too, remember?

Gods are supposed to be perfect beings on their own, which means they don't really need to reproduce. Plus, they hardly ever die.

The point of reproduction is usually to pass your genes down to future generations, right?

But gods don't have a life span, and death is a foreign concept for deities, meaning they can just carry on just fine without reproducing.

And romantic feelings are theoretically linked to reproduction, and the effect of Charmed is a status condition that appeals to those romantic feelings, sooo...

Basically, what I'm saying is that charm effects don't really work on gods...

Although a lot of the gods in Earth mythology had wild soap opera–level romantic drama.

But that's another story.

At any rate, it doesn't really affect me.

Since this thing was trying to use it on my clearly spidery clones, it must work on other species, but I think this is a bit too much of a stretch.

And even if I did have feelings like that, I wouldn't go falling for some vague shadowy silhouette striking a supposedly cool pose!

If it was at least an attractive person, the idea might've gotten across in theory, but a stupid shadow doing it just makes no sense whatsoever!

The mystery shadow, or I guess the charm shadow, keeps on striking poses for all it's worth and even tries out some dance moves eventually, but it never ends up working on me...

Honestly, watching it put on a whole show all by itself makes me feel a little bad for it.

...At any rate, it's not bothering me. I'm just gonna ignore it.

Since the multitalented shadow is just chasing my clones around and not attacking me, I'll leave that one alone for now, too.

My system-related clones have no battle abilities to speak of; they can't outrun the multitalented shadow's attacks forever.

But I've got plenty of 'em, so as long as they focus on evasion, they can at least buy some time.

It should take at least a little while for them all to get wiped out.

As long as I can attack the other shadows in the meantime and turn the tide of battle in my favor, I'll have nothing to worry about there.

Although first I'm gonna have to do something about this resurrection shadow.

And to do *that*, I have to deal with the shield shadow and the barrier shadow.

And to deal with *them*, I'm gonna have to get up close and personal, since long-distance attacks aren't getting me anywhere, but the speed shadow, thread shadow, and mist shadow all get in my way when I try to do that.

So then I try to get rid of those three first, but of course the resurrection shadow revives them…

And the circle just keeps on going around and around.

Ugh, seriously, this is the worst game ever!

Out of the three vanguard attackers, the speed shadow isn't that big of a threat.

It's certainly crazy fast, but its only attack seems to be charging in a straight line. I'm not gonna fall for something that basic.

The problem is the other two.

The thread shadow is super hard to read.

It controls ten threads, attacking in ever-changing patterns.

And it can silently deflect attacks from any angle, to the point where you start to wonder if it has eyes in the back of its head.

I don't know if these black silhouettes even have eyes, period, but let's not worry about that right now.

At the very least, given that the other shadows tend to turn their faces toward me and try to follow my movements, I'm assuming they have similar sight to normal humans.

The thread shadow seems to be the only exception.

This one has some kind of detection abilities, so it doesn't have to rely on sight.

And yet, its attack method is these thin, stupidly hard-to-see threads.

Thanks! I hate it!

On top of that, whenever I decide to just throw caution to the wind and attack the stupid thing head-on, the result is a weird attack flying at my face.

It's an invisible attack, like the kind the weirdo charm shadow uses.

Probably an Evil Eye or something, the type of ability that activates when the user can see you.

Whenever I get into the thread shadow's line of sight, I can feel my energy being slowly sapped away.

My guess is it's something like Jinx Evil Eye, which has the effect of slowly decreasing the target's HP, MP, and all-around stats.

Now that I'm a god, I don't technically have stats and all that junk anymore, but it looks like it can just directly drain my internal energy levels instead.

Because the amount lost is fairly insignificant, it's not doing much damage to speak of, but it still doesn't exactly feel great.

I end up instinctively wanting to move out of the thread shadow's line of sight, making it that much easier for the enemy to read my movements.

Since it's doing so little damage, I should just ignore it, and I really do try, but I still can't help instinctively wanting to avoid it instead.

Thanks again! I hate all of this!

And even worse, this thing can avoid Spatial Separation!

I think it's probably because it has detection abilities that don't rely on sight—it picks up on some incredibly faint premonition and avoids my attacks somehow.

So I can't take it out just by popping off an attack without thinking.

I've got to include some feints or mix it in with other attacks.

That adds an extra step to the process, giving my opponents that much more time.

But wait! There's more!

Once in a while, the thread shadow takes a hit from Spatial Separation and still doesn't die.

I have no idea how that works, but somehow, it keeps moving even with what should very obviously be fatal wounds.

When that happens, the healer shadow can fix it up from afar without the resurrection shadow needing to move. In other words, it's a huge freaking pain.

It can avoid Spatial Separation and sometimes even survive if it gets hit. Basically: I hate it!

But if I try to ignore it, I get a nonstop barrage of thread and Evil Eyes for my troubles.

I hate you! Please die!

This is the worst fight ever.

It's strong, but what's worse is that it's a kind of strength I've never encountered before.

For the most part, the toughest opponents I've faced have just been super strong, plain and simple.

Types like this, who are tricky instead of just being strong, are a lot rarer.

There are probably some humans with low stats who manage to be that tricky, but once your stats break the 10,000 mark, it's usually easier to get by with the sheer brute force of that strength.

Even a martial arts master can't take on an Aegis cruiser, know what I mean?

In which case, it'd be a whole lot easier to just get an Aegis cruiser of your own.

But this thread shadow is a rare case of something that's got Aegis cruiser strength but still fights like a martial arts master.

…Okay, even I'm not sure anymore where I was going with that example.

Anyway, on the opposite end of the tricky thread shadow, the mist shadow just relies entirely on its own strength.

Surprise attacks from its mist form.

Turning into a giant wolf and jumping at me.

Throwing punches that rely on its stupid-high stats.

Darkness-based magic attacks.

Reckless charges that depend on its own toughness and regenerative abilities.

If the thread shadow fights with the clever strategies of a human, the mist shadow fights with the raw violence of a movie monster.

More specifically, it's a vampire, really.

Its fighting style is different from Vampy's and Mera's, but its range of abilities certainly feels familiar.

Where Vampy and Mera use strategies similar to humans to maximize their power, this mist shadow is more like the pure strength of a vampire.

Like a standard-issue vampire, I guess.

Although I don't know if any vampire can really be called "standard."

Given that it's basically a monster in humanoid form, maybe it's more like the Demon Lord than Vampy or Mera.

You could say it's the tyrannical strength of stats and skills, I guess.

This one's not nearly as skillful as the thread shadow, but it's got the pure strength to make up for that difference.

Although since vampires are tricky by nature, I guess it's not quite as simple as "pure strength."

At any rate, it's undeniably strong.

The thread shadow sometimes survives Spatial Separation through what seems to be sheer force of will, but sometimes the mist shadow manages to survive, too.

In its case, though, I think it's more of a matter of just having super-high vitality and regeneration ability!

Who the hell can just stick themselves back together and heal right up when their body gets cut in half?

Sometimes it even uses that insane regeneration to straight-up charge at me without bothering to defend itself, which would be pretty damn impossible to deal with for anyone but me.

You heard me! I can still deal with it, at least!

As strong as it might be, it still doesn't hold a candle to the Demon Lord, and it might even be weaker than Vampy in a lot of ways.

It'd still pose a serious threat to any modern-day human, though.

But if it was just one on its own, I could handle it easily.

The problem is that when they team up against me, it gets a whole lot harder, even if the thread shadow and the mist shadow wouldn't be so bad one-on-one.

And to make matters worse, the speed shadow comes flying at me if I slow down for even a second.

I could forget about it all too easily if I stay focused only on the thread and mist shadows.

Plus, the endless flood of beasts from the summoner shadow is vaguely annoying, too.

They're not strong enough to be worth noting, but since there's so damn many of them, they're infuriatingly distracting.

They're like a bunch of fruit flies buzzing past my face at every turn.

What could be more annoying than that?

Without a concrete plan to resolve all these various problems, I'm doing nothing but eating up time.

But I'm not in danger of going down, either.

I know I keep griping about how strong they are, but the shadows still have far lower base specs than I do.

Their teamwork is a pain in my butthole, and they're definitely stalling my plans, but they have no real way of finishing me off.

Since I can blink all over the place with teleportation and use Spatial Separation as the ultimate defense barrier, it'd be pretty tough for these shadows to really hurt me (although I won't say it's impossible).

Even if they did manage to hurt me, I can regenerate as long as I don't run out of energy.

I used to have the Immortality skill, you know.

Even without the security of that skill now, I can still remember how it felt to be immortal.

How do you survive if all that's left is your head?

How do you regrow yourself from there?

Yep, I've already figured out those methods and learned to reproduce them.

So unless I get broken down to the atomic level, I'm not gonna die.

You call that cheating?

Fine by me!

It's a small price to pay as long as I don't die. Victory is all that matters!

All this to say that as long as the shadows don't have any other tricks up their sleeves, they can't defeat me.

And what about the other way around? Actually, I could defeat them if that was all I had to do.

You there! The reader who just thought "That's a bold claim for someone who's been dragging out this fight for pages and pages now"!

I'm not letting this fight drag on because I want to, you know!

It's true that I could defeat the shadows if it were that simple.

The problem is that I don't know what will happen to this place if I do that, which is why I haven't actually defeated them yet.

I mean, this place is super important, right? It's the heart of the system and all that. So I can't just blow up all the shadows at once! I might do serious damage to the place, that's all I'm saying…

What if I wrecked something and caused some weird error in the system?! Yeesh!

Worst-case scenario, I could even blow away the Goddess, force the system to stop and break down, and BOOM! Next thing you know, the world is destroyed!

Seriously, it could happen.

Is that scary or what?

The last thing I want is to cause a bad end after we've come all this way.

So obviously, I have to proceed with extreme caution here.

In other words, I've got to find a way to get rid of the shadows without damaging the system or the Goddess.

That's why any kind of high-powered, wide-range attack is not an option, 'cause it would also hit the Goddess and/or the system.

Even if I kept the target area limited by cranking up the power of my Dark Spears and slamming them into the shadows or something, it could still end up over penetrating a shadow and damaging the wall behind it, leading to a system failure, so I can't do that, either.

The reason I've been using Spatial Separation so much in this fight is that it's the only way I can target a precise area and still ensure high lethality.

If I didn't have to worry about causing damage to the system or the Goddess, that would definitely open up my options, but…

Hmm.

I can feel all this wasted time slipping away.

Since my movements are so limited, I've even been watching a broadcast of Team Yamada's adventures in the Great Elroe Labyrinth while I fight.

Although obviously I can't spare the attention to do anything more than take a peek.

This is a weird situation, I tell ya, being caught in this intense nonstop shootout but having nothing much to do at the same time.

It's like my own personal thousand-year war.

Okay, it hasn't actually been a thousand years, but a few days actually have passed since this battle started.

Yamada and friends are breezing right along through the Great Elroe Labyrinth, while I can't even manage to defeat a single shadow.

Which means I haven't had time to try to slow them down, either.

WAIT. Don't tell me this is also because of Divine Protection?!

Am I stuck in this super-long fight just so I won't be able to stop them?!

...Okay, that's probably overthinking it.

I'm the one who chose this moment to try and mess with the system.

I can't just blame everything on Divine Protection. That's no good.

Still, one way or another, this development certainly does work out in Team Yamada's favor.

Ugh. No waaay.

I've gotta hurry up and make a move here.

Hrm.

Looks like these shadows never run out of steam...

Usually, anyone would lose momentum of some kind after fighting for this long.

You'd run out of stamina or magic or something like that.

Even I'm no exception—I can't fight forever.

In my case, I've got tons of stored-up energy, and I'm being careful to conserve it as much as possible, which is how I've been able to keep it up for so long.

Not to mention that I can't use any big moves in this room, forcing me to hold back.

The shadows, on the other hand, clearly must be going all-out.

Especially the speed shadow—it's been going full throttle nonstop.

Yet somehow, they've been recklessly running at full power for days now.

Considering how strong these shadows are, it makes some sense that they'd be able to fight at full strength for a full day or so.

But several days in a row? Come on now.

They should definitely be getting winded at this point.

Since they haven't, though, I should probably assume that they're getting unlimited backup from the system.

That would explain why they seem to have full MP and SP at all times.

I allowed myself to get drawn into this long battle because I was hoping they would wear themselves out, but if that's not gonna happen, I'll have to change my approach.

I need to break out of this deadlock, even if I have to be a little more forceful than I'd like.

Especially since that multitalented shadow has whittled down the number of system-related clones quite a bit.

Once they're all gone, it'll probably join in attacking me next...

Would that mean curtains for me? I don't think so, but it'd make things even more of a pain than they already are.

And there's one more reason I want to finish this as quickly as possible, too.

If the shadows are getting backup from the system, that means the system is supplying them in energy—which means the longer we fight, the more they waste the energy we've saved up in the system.

The shadows probably aren't using a huge amount of energy for this battle, but it's still being wasted, no matter how small the amount.

That's energy we collected by igniting a huge war and letting countless people die in battle.

I can't have that being lost.

After all the sacrifices that created these energy stores, it would be wrong to let any more of it go to waste in this meaningless fight.

So let's hurry up and end it.

...That being said, what am I gonna do, exactly?

I could easily wipe out all the shadows in one go, sure.

The problem is how to do it without causing any damage to the system or the Goddess.

Idea number one: Use a big wide-range blast to destroy them all and hope it doesn't cause any extra damage.

Nope.

It'd be way too dangerous to bet everything on a risky move full of unknown variables when failure could potentially result in the end of the whole world.

Would the system really break so easily? Probably not, but the Goddess is already gone from the waist down and looking like the rest of her could vanish at any moment now.

By all appearances, she seems so weakened that a single stray missile hitting her by mistake might put her at death's door.

If I killed her by such a stupid accident, I could never look the Demon Lord in the eye again.

Idea number two: Slowly increase the firepower of my attacks and finish off the resurrection shadow once it outclasses the defenses of the shield and barrier shadows.

This plan sounds fairly practical, but it'd actually be pretty tough to pull off...

Conjuring and magic are fairly similar.

I mean, even the magic system itself is just one big conjuring anyway.

In that way, you could say that magic is a part of conjuring.

Just like magic, conjuring requires construction, which is basically the blueprints for a spell.

You create a rune according to a pattern and fill it with energy to activate the conjuring.

Now, those blueprints actually predetermine how strong the attack is gonna be and stuff like that.

If you try to make a building bigger by just taking the blueprints and scaling 'em up as-is, for instance, it's probably not gonna go very well.

Because when you change the size of the building, you have to change stuff like the size of the support beams, the materials, and all that jazz.

In the same way, if you want to make a conjuring stronger, you have to alter the construction.

Usually, that holds true for magic, too, but back when I had the support of the Height of Occultism skill, I could mostly change things up however I wanted.

But now that I don't have Height of Occultism, I have to do those kinds of alterations manually.

And that's not exactly easy.

If I just have to let loose a bunch of constructions I've already completed, it's still not simple per se, but I've gotten the hang of it over these past few years by training myself.

Like I keep saying, constructions for conjurings are basically like blueprints: You assemble the runes in accordance with the blueprints, then fill them with energy to activate them.

If you make the same thing over and over and fill it with the same amount of energy every time, eventually, you'll memorize even the smallest details and get that much faster at completing it.

It's like that thing where people practice putting together a gun that's been broken down into parts, loading it with bullets, and pulling the trigger.

Guns always have a set amount of firepower, too.

Solid example, if I do say so myself.

If you want to make it stronger, you'd have to start by going back to the drawing board and reconsidering the fundamental structure of the gun itself.

Frankly, it's a huge pain.

If I really want to, I can tweak the power a little bit, you know?

But only very roughly.

Since I don't know how much power it would take to bust through my opponents' defenses, I would have to adjust my firepower very carefully.

But right now, all I can do is really broad changes—like going from a pistol to a rifle, a bazooka, and then a wave cannon.

That's the best I can do with the conjurings I have on hand.

If I was gonna do it, I think the best way would be to try to slowly raise the power of my Dark Spears, but that would be like gradually increasing the amount of gunpowder you put into the bullets of a pistol.

Something's bound to explode sooner or later...

But changing the conjuring itself would be like trying to turn a pistol into a rifle.

And if I shoot them with a rifle, and it ends up being too strong and plows right through and into the Goddess...

If I reeeally took my time altering the construction of my Dark Spears and testing things out, I do think it's theoretically possible, but that could end up taking ages...

Yeah, let's table that idea, too.

Idea number three: Summon some battle clones.

If I brought in the battle clones here, I could wipe out these stupid shadows with the strength of numbers.

There's twelve of them, but I could call in waaay more than that and probably win with ease.

This method would be the easiest and most guaranteed way to wipe out the shadows.

I just have two concerns here.

One, because of my own mental capacity, I would have to temporarily stop all my information-gathering clones to concentrate on moving the battle clones.

Believe it or not, there is a limit to how many clones I can control at the same time, despite how amazingly awesome I am.

So for whatever amount of battle clones I bring in, I would have to stop managing the same amount of information-gathering clones.

On that note, the multitalented shadow has taken out a few of my system-related clones, freeing up a few of those spaces.

Plus, as long as I can wipe out all the shadows in a short period of time, I don't have to stop the spy clones for too long.

And I can choose which ones to shut down from places that I probably don't need to watch too closely.

So this one isn't actually that big of a deal.

It's the other concern that might be really serious.

But it might end up being an unfounded worry, too...

This might not sound super important, but basically, I've got a sneaking suspicion about something.

Namely: If I bring in reinforcements, won't they do the same thing?

I mean, these guys totally look like mass-produced goods, y'know?

When you actually fight them, each of the shadows has totally unique individual abilities, but who could tell that at a glance?

They all look the same, except maybe the resurrection shadow being kinda pudgy.

And given how cookie-cutter they look, who's to say they can't just pop out more?

And who says that won't be exactly what happens when they see that I'm bringing in enemy reinforcements from their point of view?

I mean, ramping up your forces to match the number of enemies is just common sense in battle.

I could try summoning just one to see what happens, but I'm afraid to do that in case they immediately double in number or something.

Hopefully I'm overthinking it, and these are the only shadows they have in store.

But this defense mechanism was created by D, sooo...

You never know what might happen.

It's kind of impressive that she's so dependably untrustworthy.

This could even turn into an all-out war between my clones and the shadows...

What a creepy image...

But this is the most realistic plan I've come up with so far, and as long as there aren't any more shadows lying in wait, it'd be an easy win.

Hmm, hmm, hmmmm...

Well, just worrying about it won't get me anywhere, so maybe I should just go for broke and summon a clone?

But I guess I spent too long thinking about it, because suddenly, the speed shadow is right on top of me.

Oh shit.

It's actually gonna hit me.

Without thinking at all, I throw out my arm in a totally instinctive reaction.

That's not gonna stop it from crashing into me...

But then the impact I'm expecting never comes, and instead, I can feel the weight of something being clutched in the hand I thrust out toward the shadow.

Oh, I see. It's a giant white scythe.

I kinda forgot I had this thing...

I crafted this scythe with the blade of one of my own front legs before I became a god. Then when that whole thing happened, it absorbed some of the energy from a bomb that could theoretically destroy an entire continent.

It's made from part of me, and it basically underwent deification along with me.

Which might be why it sometimes ignores my wishes and does stupid crap like this.

Admittedly, most of the time, that "stupid crap" happens to involve saving my ass when I need it the most, but still.

I definitely get the impression that this thing has a mind of its own. It's not just my imagination, right?

Even right now, it's totally giving off a smug aura, somehow.

I guess that's fair, though.

Since it just magically appeared in my hour of need, rescued me from a tight spot, and totally blew away the speed shadow to boot.

Yep...

It blasted away the shadow that was charging right toward me...

Without a trace, in fact...

Well, yeah, I guess this scythe has always had some Rot attribute–like effect.

Rot is a super-dangerous attribute that obliterates the target to the point where not a speck of dust remains. For example, it slew Julius the hero without leaving any room for resistance.

I guess even these shadows don't stand a chance against it.

And no new shadow has appeared to immediately replace their fallen comrade.

Maybe the arrival of the scythe didn't count as reinforcements, or maybe there were never any backup shadows to begin with.

Either way, now that I've got a weapon that can destroy my opponents instantly, there's no need to summon clones at all.

Okay, time to hack these guys to pieces!

I charge straight for the mist shadow and swing my scythe.

The shadow seems to know that a hit from this scythe would be bad news, and it turns into mist to try to flee.

Bwa-ha-ha-ha!

You wish, pal!

Turning into mist, which is basically just really fine particles, probably means most attacks won't hit you.

But here's the thing!

Rot attribute is an insta-kill attack, you know?

No matter how finely you split yourself up, all it has to do is touch one part of you, and death will spread throughout the rest of your entire body.

The scythe cuts right through the fog-like mist shadow, scattering it into nothingness.

Hot damn.

Is this weapon OP or what?

I haven't used it lately since it tends to be a bit overkill, but this scythe sure is strong.

Looks like it should be smooth sailing (or slicing) from here on out.

The thread shadow is next.

Ten threads shoot toward me—but I'm a thread user, too.

I know all about the many ways of attacking with threads.

Fending them off is no problem for me.

In fact, all I really need to do is mow them down with my scythe, easy-peasy.

I slice right through the threads and close in on the thread shadow itself.

Just as it seems to look right at me, I feel a strange sensation throughout my body.

…Looks like it did something to me.

I resisted whatever it was, though.

It was probably a last-ditch Evil Eye, but I resist it easily and strike home with my scythe.

If that shadow had some kind of Rot-based Evil Eye move, it might've been a closer call.

I'm guessing the recoil from something like that would kill the user, too, but all it would need to do is have the resurrection shadow bring it back.

Then you could easily get into a terrifying pattern of self-destruction via Rot-attribute Evil Eye, resurrect, and rinse and repeat.

That probably would've been dangerous even for me.

My scythe is proof enough of how scary the Rot attribute is, after all.

At any rate, that's it for the vanguard shadows.

Now I just need to take care of the rear guard—but then the multitalented shadow changes targets and comes after me instead.

It starts wildly shooting magic at me and sending each of the rainbow of floating weapons toward me one after another.

But while it's got a lot of moves, none of them are all that strong on their own.

It's basically just for show.

I easily fend off the magic and weapons coming my way, then slice through the multitalented shadow itself with my scythe.

Its body falls apart in two halves, then vanishes within seconds.

Oh-ho-ho.

So much for all the trouble you guys were giving me before!

Man, this feels great…

Guess I built up a lot of stress over the course of this battle that's gone on for way too long.

It's so refreshing to slaughter these enemies in one blow!

Yeah, I could get used to this…

All right, next, it's finally your turn! Resurrection shadow!

I locate my target and run forward.

The shield shadow and barrier shadow are standing in my way, but that doesn't matter now!

One swing, two swings.

That's all it takes for the shield and barrier shadows to disappear.

Now all that's left is the resurrection shadow standing there defenseless.

You sure made this whole thing a lot harder for me, didn't ya?!

Bwa-ha-ha. Excuse me, please die!

I bring down my scythe.

Then a different figure pushes the resurrection shadow aside.

It's the charm shadow, which has been putting on a pointless one-man show of cool poses this whole time.

Wow. It sacrificed itself to save the resurrection shadow.

It's been totally useless the whole time, but it really went and pulled off some manly heroics at the last second, huh?

Too bad I'm just gonna swing my scythe right back and get the resurrection shadow, too.

Cruel?

Look, I know it's sad, but that's war for you.

Sometimes you just gotta mercilessly slaughter enemy soldiers!

Now all that's left is the healer, summoner, and commander shadows, plus the last one that still hasn't moved from its designated spot in front of the Goddess.

The former three are all gathered in one place, so I guess I'll take them out first.

But then, before I have a chance to approach them, that last one finally makes its move instead.

Since this scythe landed in my hand, I've been acting like I've got this in the bag, but I better check myself before I wreck myself.

Somehow, I just get the feeling that I should be extra careful of this last guy.

The last shadow holds out its hand toward me.

A bad feeling prickles my skin.

Ooh, this thing's definitely trouble...

I brace myself.

And then, the last shadow shoots a beam of light out of its hand!

Well, shit!

That's some crazy-concentrated energy coming right at me!

Even I won't escape unscathed if I get hit by that!

I gotta dodge—wait, no!

If I move aside, it'll hit the wall behind me!

Then it might damage the system!

If you're supposed to be the system's defense mechanism, why are you using attacks that could easily hurt it?!

I brace myself and get ready to intercept it.

Holding my scythe out in front of me, I slash through the beam with its blade.

A heavy impact ripples through my hands.

The scythe's Rot power and the beam's intense energy are clashing, canceling each other out.

I grip the handle tightly, pushing back to make sure my scythe doesn't get knocked aside.

Ngh!

What kind of insane energy levels must this thing be putting out that it can resist the powers of my scythe?!

This is way too different from the other shadows!

Shoot, my hands are going numb...

Right before I hit my limit, the beam finally stops.

Phew, thank goodness.

If it had gone on for one more second, my scythe was about to slip right out of my hand.

Then I would've taken a direct hit from the beam, and I bet it would've blown my body to bits.

That was waaay too close.

Once it stops emitting the beam, the last shadow doesn't take a defensive stance—it just collapses on the spot.

Its body fades into nothing.

Wait, did that guy just put all the energy that comprised its own body into that beam of light?

Yikes, that's a scary move...

It was crazy strong, for sure, but I dunno about throwing your life away in a literal one-shot suicide attack like that...

Now I know why that shadow didn't move until the last minute.

If it used its attack, it would die. That's why it waited for the crucial moment.

Rot Attack generally kills the user, too, but if you converted even your body into energy and fired it like that, doesn't that mean your soul would get used up, too?

If so, that's even scarier than the backlash from Rot Attack.

If your soul disappears, you can't get resurrected, and you can't even reincarnate.

With an attack that serious, no wonder it got so dangerously close to doing me in.

Offering up your entire self in one decisive attack to vanquish the enemy.

It could probably only do that because it was a shadow and not a human...

If any human was capable of that same feat, they'd have to be a little bit crazy, I think.

Well, that was a bigger attack than I expected, but now there's only three left.

Might as well clean 'em up, since I doubt they've got any more tricks up their sleeves now.

I wipe out the swarm of beasts charging at me with a single slash and take down the summoner shadow.

The healer shadow and commander shadow can't do anything on their own, so I take them down easily, too.

Just like that, the long battle against the shadows is finally over.

Now I'm hacking the system along with the surviving system-related clones.

That multitalented shadow reduced their numbers quite a bit.

I'm gonna have to make more...

I'd like to do that right away, but picking these locks takes priority.

Carefully, I pick the closed locks and pry them open, one by one.

So far, nothing has popped up to stop me.

I was honestly a little worried that more shadows would appear once I defeated those ones, but it doesn't look like that's going to happen.

I guess once you defeat the shadows, that's it for the defense mechanism.

Maybe it would've been safe to summon my battle clones after all.

But no point dwelling on that now.

It all worked out anyway, since I was able to win without them thanks to the scythe.

Maybe I should have used this thing against Julius the hero, too?

...No, I think I made the right choice back then. We couldn't risk anything going wrong in that situation.

I used a Rot-attribute Evil Eye attack to kill Julius.

It's an insta-kill attack, just like my scythe.

An incredibly powerful one that can kill someone just by looking at them.

But it comes at a pretty high cost.

My eyes are still damaged from using it.

The damage is so deep that not even my regenerative abilities can easily fix it.

I can use things like X-ray vision and telescopic vision, but I'm trying to hold off on using Evil Eyes style abilities; it's not that I absolutely can't use them, but I think it would slow down the healing process.

It's gotten a lot better already, and I think I should be fully recovered by the time we get to the elf village even if I use an Evil Eye or two, but there's no harm in being extra careful.

That's also why I didn't use any in the battle against the shadows.

I was only willing to pay that high price because the existence of the hero is just that terrifying.

On top of the obvious danger to the Demon Lord, he had the potential to kill even a god like me with that Sword of the Hero.

The fact that we couldn't get him to waste it against the Queen clone is a serious blow.

Hyrince said he'd get rid of the Sword of the Hero, so I gave it to him, but it somehow still seems to have ended up at Yamada's waist?

Um, helloooo?

Hyrince gave it to the third prince Leston as Julius the hero's last request, and then Leston passed it on to Yamada as part of Julius's will in turn.

He at least honored his promise not to reveal the nature of Julius's Sword of the Hero to anyone else and didn't explain it to Yamada, but still.

Leston is all well and good.

But Hyrince, what are you doing handing off such a dangerous thing to other people?!

That thing would work on me or even the real you, y'know!

What the hell was he thinking...?

Or did all that happen because of Divine Protection, too?!

Did it activate just to make sure Yamada got a powerful weapon?!

Ugh, no, that's dumb.

I refuse to believe it.

Otherwise, my "Divine Protection is all-powerful" theory would actually be true.

I don't know what Hyrince's motive was, but it sure makes it a hell of a lot more dangerous to risk interfering with Yamada myself.

I guess that might even be why he did it—to make sure I don't try anything too overt on Yamada and his friends.

Well, I suppose I can't blame him for being wary of me, since I did murder Julius with my own hands.

If only I had succeeded in getting rid of the hero feature, this would all be a lot easier.

I leave the system-related clones in charge of all the work for a moment and walk up to the Goddess.

<Proficiency has reached the required level.>

<Experience has reached the required level.>

<Proficiency has reached the required level.>

Her mouth isn't moving, yet her voice echoes endlessly throughout the room.

All of the world's system messages, from level-ups to skill-ups, are sent out to every individual from this room.

The voice that relays these notices sounds flat and emotionless.

I always assumed that the Goddess had her thoughts and emotions stolen away while she's bound to the system, rendering her a perfectly silent sacrifice.

But what if that's not true…?

I open my eyes and look at the Goddess's face.

When I killed Julius, my system-related clones were attacked by the shadows of the defense mechanism here just like I was before.

They had no way of defending themselves against the shadows, of course; by the time I arrived in person, the next hero had already been assigned, and my attempt to get rid of the hero function ended in failure.

Since there was no point sticking it out once my plan failed, I just gathered my system-related clones and withdrew.

Then, once the shadows went away, I sent the system-related clones back in.

Nothing about that sequence of events seemed particularly strange.

If the system's defense mechanism was set up that way in advance, that reaction makes perfect sense.

But something about it doesn't quite feel right to me.

Specifically: Yamada himself.

Yamada being chosen as the new hero seems way too good to be true.

He's a reincarnation, has the extraordinary Divine Protection skill, and is even the biological younger brother of the previous hero.

When you think about it that way, sure, he seems perfectly suited to be the new hero.

And his appointment certainly did cause plenty of extra work for us on the Demon Lord side.

Surely, no one could be a better hero than that.

But is that really true, though?

I started to have my doubts when I asked about the history of heroes and demon lords past.

Because normally, when a hero or demon lord dies and the title is passed on to the next, the new one *isn't* chosen directly after the previous holder dies.

There's a delay, albeit a short one, while the system determines who is best suited to be the next hero or demon lord.

It's because of that delay that the Demon Lord was able to use her ruler privileges to refuse that assignment so many times, before finally accepting it and becoming the demon lord this time around.

In other words, there was enough delay for the Demon Lord to have the opportunity to choose.

But that didn't happen in Yamada's case.

I know this because I was monitoring Yamada through a clone even as I killed Julius the hero.

Yamada became the hero at almost the exact moment Julius died.

The delay that normally occurred was completely absent.

Which makes me suspect that someone decided of their own volition that Yamada would be the next hero.

But who could have done that?

There are only two possible contenders.

D, or the Goddess here...

If it was D, that's fine.

Knowing that voyeuristic personality, she might've chosen Yamada purely because it seemed entertaining.

But what if D wasn't the culprit?

If that was the case, then I'd be a little pissed about it.

I throw my fist toward the Goddess's face.

But then I change my mind at the last second and stop right in front of her.

...I don't know for sure if that's true.

To think that the Goddess would ignore the feelings of the Demon Lord, who's been working herself to the bone trying to save the very same Goddess, and make Yamada the hero on purpose...no, that can't possibly be the case.

Yeah, I'm just gonna pray that it's not true.

Pray to the Goddess, as it were.

I draw back my hand, turn my back on the Goddess, and teleport away.

SARIEL

Real name unknown. The Word of God religion considers her the voice of god, and the Goddess religion worships Sariel herself. Ariel seems to see her as a mother. Before the system was created, she warned humanity of the dangers of MA energy. But they ignored her, and the world was driven to the brink of destruction. In order to prevent that, humanity offered her up as a sacrifice, and she became the nucleus of the world. She is held in the very bottom of the Great Elroe Labyrinth, constantly running the system. She sends the messages that White uses to call the Divine Voice (temp.) to everyone in the world.

Interlude   ???

I don't know where I am.

A vast, empty space.

And a woman is here with me.

Her body is disappearing, like it's melting into the space, leaving only part of her upper body behind.

It's heartrending to witness.

Then mechanical words spill from her mouth.

<Proficiency has reached the required level.>

<Experience has reached the required level.>

<Proficiency has reached the required level.>

....

<It hurts.>

My eyes flash open, and I jerk upright.

...So it was just a dream?

Final Chapter

DESTROYING THE ELVES FOR A LIVING

For some reason, I suddenly felt like I couldn't be in that room any longer, and I popped over here.

Well, it seemed like the system-related clones could handle the rest of the work. No big deal.

In fact, I don't have much choice but to leave it to them...

It seems like it's going to take a long time to pick those locks, huh...?

Maybe I underestimated how involved it would be.

But as my absence doesn't do much except maybe lessen their efficiency a little, I might as well just let the system-related clones take their time breaking open all those locks.

I've got a big job ahead of me right now, after all.

"So it's finally time."

The Demon Lord gazes ahead of us, murmuring quietly.

As the demon army advances, disguised as the imperial army, we can already see our destination in the distance.

A huge forest.

The Great Garam Forest.

The village of the elves is hidden within those trees.

Up ahead, the imperial army has already entered the forest.

They're moving slowly, since they're cutting down trees and branches as they advance to clear an easier path.

It shouldn't be long before the demon army catches up to the imperial army.

And by the time that happens, we should reach the elf village shortly thereafter.

It's time.

At long last, the time has come to settle things with Potimas.

In the end, Yamada and friends made it to the elf village in time without a hitch, despite my efforts.

Depending on how the unknown factor of Team Yamada comes into play, the flow of the battle will probably change.

But this much I can say for sure:

"It's all over for Potimas."

"Heh. You're right." The Demon Lord smiles and nods. "Yes, it's been a long, long time. Let's finally put an end to that story."

"Yeah."

Now, time for the first big step in our plan to save the world.

Let's get rid of the malignant parasite called Potimas. He's leeched off this world for too long.

"Shall we go, then?"

"Yeah."

Afterword

Is everyone doing well?! I certainly am!

Yes, hello, I'm Okina Baba, doing well as usual.

This is Volume 13.

The number thirteen is considered unlucky, and this year certainly has been that kind of year…

In my case, since I'm an author, I can still work from home, so that wasn't particularly a problem.

Fortunately, no one in my family has gotten the illness. I can't say it's been peaceful, but we've been getting by.

But while I've still been able to write, it's not as if it hasn't affected me at all. There have been a handful of unexpected obstacles.

The local bookstore was voluntarily closed for a while, for instance…

And because this is all so unprecedented, the industry itself has been fumbling, too.

All I can really do to help is keep on writing as best I can, though.

I hope I can bring people even a little bit of energy with my books.

Now, a few thank-yous.

To Tsukasa Kiryu for such wonderful illustrations as always.

Even in this situation—no, *especially* because of this situation—looking at Kiryu's artwork soothes my soul more than ever!

When I see those illustrations, I feel like I can keep on going.

To Asahiro Kakashi, who draws the manga adaptation.

Again, when I see the manga version of the protagonist doing her best, whether the situation is comical or serious, I'm inspired to do my best, too.

And Gratinbird, who's handling the spin-off comic.

Reading the absurd hijinks of the four sisters makes me smile, warms my heart, and puts me in a happy mood.

I hope this volume will make all of you readers feel the same... Erm...will it, though?

...Look, I can't imitate Gratinbird's sense of humor!

And to everyone involved in the anime adaptation.

Because anime production involves so many people, I think it's hurt all the more by the effects of the recent coronavirus outbreak.

Since the staff all keeps working hard, I feel like I've got to work hard, too.

And speaking of the anime, we've got a huge announcement!

It's going to air in January 2021 as a back-to-back two-hour broadcast!

It was originally supposed to air in 2020, but it got delayed to 2021 because of that damned corona...

It's certainly been an eventful year, but please wait a little longer for the broadcast!

I also want to thank my editor, Ms. W, and everyone else who helped bring this book into the world.

And all of you who were kind enough to pick up this book.

Thank you very much.

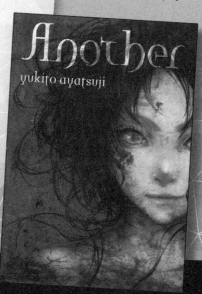